SHADOW WATCHER

Darkness Series #6

K.F. BREENE

SYNOPSIS

In the wake of ridding their territory of a menace, Sasha has only one pressing duty left: find more human magic workers. And while it is undoubtedly important on some grand scale, the task is, in itself, surprisingly uneventful. That is, until a strange predator takes an interest in her and Charles on their trek home one evening. In the space of twenty-four hours Sasha's life goes from mundane to being stalked and threatened. A new shifter has moved into town, and if the whispered rumors are true, something even more sinister is lurking behind, watching and waiting for the right moment to spring.

But that isn't the only element that turns Sasha's life upside down. She has one hell of a secret that will change her and Stefan's life forever.

ACKNOWLEDGEMENTS

Thank you to all the fans that have made the series a success. As some of you know, this book was written solely for all of you. The contents, names of the new additions, and other items were picked out by the fans. This is my thanks to you!

I'd also like to thank the beta readers, who helped this along: Keri Frey and Heather Kuebler. And the proof readers who came in at the last minute and tried to find every error they could: Brianna Tesar, Tina Tame, Kelly Degenhardt, Nikki Holcomb, Raven Click, Donna Hokanson and Paula Sadler. Last, thank you to my new editor, Steve Lockley, who is aghast I go through life with such little knowledge of the English language.

ALSO BY K.F. BREENE

Never want to miss the latest? Sign up here!

CHAPTER ONE

"*S*o we think these people are supposed to notice us, right?" Charles kicked a stone that clattered into the street. He wasn't hiding his boredom well.

We waited outside a New Age shop in the middle of town. The window display of crystals, Tarot cards, and other mystical treasures was designed to lure in humans that thought they had magic of some sort—or those that just wanted to dabble in magic. Most of the patrons were women, but the occasional man with long straggly hair and smelling of patchouli oil wandered through.

"Notice you. I think this gig has made me judgmental," I noted, leaning against the wall.

We waited in a shadowed corner as the sun sank low in the sky. Long, jagged shadows reached across the sidewalk, as though searching for something or someone. Streetlights had started to blink on even though they weren't needed yet. The bite of fall had me shivering through my light sweatshirt and huddling into Charles.

I watched the people meander by, enjoying the pleasant evening in twos and threes. A few glanced my way, noticing me by the wall like a creeper. A guy or two even gave me a smile. They didn't notice Charles, even though we were touching. Some of these people passed within a few feet of him and even though he was the largest man on the street they still didn't see him. It was as if he was wearing an invisibility blanket. People's gazes slid right past as they continued on their way.

I gave a loud sigh, which drew the attention of an aging man with a walker. I slouched harder against the wall. This had become my gig lately. With things so quiet in our neck of the woods since we'd taken down Andris, I set about my other duty of continuing Fate's plan and finding humans with magic. I was blending the two sides of magic together to save the magical race.

Or so Cato said every time he called. Which was often.

I had found three people so far, all of them old women. They'd had some control over their magic and no idea of what they might be capable of. While they didn't have a lot of power, I had a little hope that they could at least join the fold and find some of the hidden traits we needed. Delilah wasn't blasting orange like Birdie, but there was no one better at working intricate spells. I was improving in leaps and bounds by practicing with her, and now I knew how to link without killing people—learning wasn't nearly the dangerous activity it used to be.

The old women hadn't worked out. They had spent no more than fifteen minutes in the Mansion before turning around and marching right back out. Apparently orgies weren't their thing.

"I don't understand why Jonas and I can't switch off on this detail. It's boring, Sasha," Charles whined. "I'm all edgy. I want to stab something. Or at least punch someone in the face. It's never been this boring around you before. Let's go to the ghetto and parade you around topless so I have an excuse to kill someone who hits on you."

"Super idea, Charles," I said, "Let's go do that right now."

"Really?" Charles' eyes sparkled as he looked down at me.

"No, you idiot. And you'd want me topless just so you could see my wares. You're not very sneaky."

"Win-win. Your breasts and violence." Charles slapped the wall. The sound reverberated into the ambling crowd. I made eye contact with the few people who were trying to find the origin of the noise and almost didn't notice a man look directly at Charles.

A thrill went through my body. We got one!

I zeroed in on the guy. Standing over six feet and stacked with muscle, the man was in his mid-twenties and owned his space. He created a sphere of emptiness around him despite the busy sidewalk. Tattoos wound around his arms and reached out of his collar to his neck. A wicked scar curved at the base of his jaw but didn't diminish the handsomeness in his face. What it did was amplify the scary quality of a violent nature. He walked with a swagger that revealed a physical confidence born of fighting. Muscular arms hung from broad shoulders and swung freely at his sides, ready to grapple at a moment's notice. His eyes seemed haunted, but there had been no fear when he had looked at Charles. There was no sign of a challenge, but certainly not submissive.

The thrill turned into the warning tingle. Why me?

"We got one," I groaned.

"Which one?" Charles asked, staring at a portly woman who was walking out of the shop.

"No, not the woman who looks like she wouldn't harm a fly. That would be a good thing. Nope. The huge, scary-looking guy who Jonas will probably want to kill on sight."

"I changed my mind. I love this detail." Charles had

followed my gaze and was now looking at the man with glee. Which meant my assessment was right on.

Just great.

"Jesus. That guy's big for a human." Charles rubbed his hands together with a grin. "Ready for a tumble, too. I'm his huckleberry."

I rolled my eyes. "When you quote a movie, you don't have to try and sound like the character."

"Sounds better that way."

It didn't, but I didn't say that. The man was getting away.

I pushed myself away from the wall and slipped into the stream of passers-by with Charles at my side. We walked quickly until we were a few paces behind the guy, then slowed to match his leisurely pace. He looked straight ahead for the most part, but by the tightening of his shoulders and the flexing of his arms, I was sure that he knew there was something dangerous behind him. He had great instincts.

As if hearing my assessment, Charles muttered, "He's a born fighter. I bet he'd be trouble for any human he came across."

"And you?"

"Don't be an idiot, Sasha. I'd rock his world."

Ego. The man had it in spades.

"We need to get him alone. If we stop him here, he'll probably throw a punch. He obviously knows you can fight, or he wouldn't be getting all puffed up."

"How long did he look at me?" Charles rolled his massive shoulders. He was preparing for trouble.

"Just a moment, but it was enough. He sized you up immediately. Either that or he already knew what you were..." I elbowed Charles as he flexed his fingers. "We aren't trying to fight him, you moron. The last thing I need is people watching a human fighting with empty air. Or seeing me do magic. I don't want to see the inside of a lab any more than Tim does."

"Tim turns into a bear. You don't. You wouldn't go to a lab, you'd go to a mental institution."

"Oh, well, that makes me feel much better."

The man slowed as he approached an alleyway. I put my hand on Charles' bicep as the man veered off the sidewalk and into the murky gray. Shadows reached out, wrapping him in their tight embrace before sucking him in and masking his body.

My fingers tightened around Charles' arm. "Did you see that? Did you see the way the shadows grabbed for him?"

"Yeah, so? C'mon, he's getting away."

"Charles, shadows don't do that with humans. They do that with your kind."

Charles gave me a puzzled look before dragging me toward the alleyway. "You're just getting worked up because you sense the danger. Relax, I got this covered. He's big for a human, but small for my crew. He's not one of us. And unless he's a freak like you, he can't throw magic. We're good."

"What if he's got…friends?" I gulped as we stepped into the dark of the alley. I could do magic, yes. Failing that, I could run fast. But these situations still made me nervous until I knew what I was up against.

I felt Charles' hand on my back, guiding me into the murky pools of shadow. The edges of shapes hazed as deep colors blended into the darkness. Light from distant street-lights caught only patches of the garbage-strewn ground.

Squinting didn't provide any more definition. I relied on Charles' guidance as his eyes adapted well to the night while I willed my own to adjust faster. The guy could be waiting in there, hiding only a step away. Hell, a small army could be in there somewhere and I wouldn't notice them until they jumped out and yelled, "Boo!"

"Up there." Charles directed me to the right side of the alleyway. There, in a pool of dark beside a dumpster, lurked a large shape. I could barely see something metallic in his hand.

"Gun," I said in a quick release of breath.

Charles pushed me against the grimy wall and shielded me with his body, but my magic was already in full flow. I shot off a spell to wrap the man's body in tight black bands. As my shoulder scraped the wall I yanked the magic taught, trapping the man's arms to his sides and sending the gun clattering to the ground.

"What the fuck?" the man roared in an angry rasp.

"Okay, we're good," I mumbled into Charles' back. "Get off!"

As soon as Charles was out of the way I approached the dumpster. The hazy glow from the streetlight wasn't enough light for me to make out the man's features, but it didn't take a genius to know he was freaked out. Unless he'd seen all this before, and was afraid of what we were about to do to him.

I glanced at the sky and then the ground. I pointed to a brighter patch of light a short distance away. "Move him over there, Charles."

"Why?" Charles was staring at the man.

"So I can see. I don't have raccoon eyes like you do."

Charles stepped forward and bent so his eyes were at the same level as the man's. "Stay calm, human, and this won't hurt."

The man didn't flinch when Charles lifted him off the ground then set him down where I'd indicated. He didn't complain, either. Or struggle. He didn't pay much attention to Charles at all. His attention was fixed on me. No matter where I moved, his focus always stayed on me.

These weren't the reactions of a normal human. I should know—I had reacted much differently when I met Charles for the first time. This guy might be human, but he wasn't what he seemed.

Steady, Sasha, don't jump to conclusions too quickly.

I tried to keep the accusation from my voice. "Do you have magic?"

The man continued to stare as if he was waiting for something.

I glanced around looking for the hidden army that might be about to try to save him.

Nothing.

What the hell was he waiting for? A rabbit to appear?

"Do you know how I am holding you prisoner?" I demanded. "Is that why you're so calm? You've been through this before?"

The man continued to stare. It was starting to get irritating.

"Maybe he's already had a run-in with Jonas," Charles suggested.

"I doubt he'd be this calm if he'd had a run-in with Jonas. If he even remembered it."

I walked right up to Charles as he picked up the gun. "Looks like a throw-away," Charles observed. "The serial number has been scratched off."

I put my hands on my hips in frustration and stared at the handsome man. I knew my eyebrows were furrowed and my lips were in a thin line, but I couldn't help it—he wasn't acting normal, damn it, and I wanted to know why.

"What's your deal? Have you seen people like Charles before?" I threw a thumb in Charles' direction.

"Human male, I'd answer her. She's starting to get annoyed. You want to be on the move when she gets all crazy, trust me."

"Not helping, Charles."

"What do you want?" the man rasped, still staring down at me.

"Who are you?" I asked.

My question was met with silence.

"Have you seen people like Charles before?" I tried again.

I got the same frustrating response—a deadpan stare and no movement in the mouth.

I barely kept from stomping my foot in exasperation. "Dude, you're not going anywhere until you've answered a few simple questions. Just tell me why you're acting strange and we'll settle this. I don't want to have to make you talk..."

I let the threat linger, hovering in the air. I didn't actually plan to hurt him, but he didn't know that. The threat of pain was often a powerful motivator.

His expression didn't change but a wildness had crept into his eyes at my warning. A fire flickered and then roared to life. A subtle change took hold of him and his muscles flexing down his sizable frame.

He did not like being threatened. He was ready to answer my challenge with a primal energy I rarely saw in humans.

That's when I noticed it. When I really looked at the guy.

Underneath the rough exterior, this guy was striking in a familiar way. His bearing, poise and physical development indicated someone in their mid-to-early thirties, but his face looked like he was only in his mid-twenties. His body was fit, with the large shoulders, defined pecs and loose shirt around the middle indicated a flat stomach, but it was also fluid and graceful, like a dancer. His grace and agility was natural. He was born with the ability to fight, but he'd learned to control the consuming need for violence, I'd bet my life on it. He was a predator at home in the shadows.

"Oh my God," I breathed. My stomach rolled with implications. "Who are your parents?"

The fire boiled over and turned his face into a mask of

anger. His body straining against my magic. I felt him pulling at the elements. He was yanking at them to help him fight and to break free. I was right. I knew I was!

"Look, bitch," he seethed. "I ain't got no money and I ain't with Jimmy's crew no more. I got no ties. I got nothin'. So what the fuck do you want?"

"Ohhh, he's feisty." Charles moved in close ready to defend me. "You sure you got him wrapped up tight?"

"You do have access to your magic. But you think you're a freak, right?" I asked in a hush. "You see people lurking in the shadows that no one else can see, right? Have any followed you before?"

The man's jaw clenched.

I tapped Charles. "Make your arms glow."

I felt Charles pull at his magic. The runes on his arms seared into life. The man's eyes glanced at the runes and then back at my face with no sign of surprise.

Oh yeah, this guy had secrets. And I knew exactly which ones. Wanna see that rabbit?

"Seen a few people like him, huh?" I gave him a knowing smile. "You see people like him lingering in the shadows, right? Moving through the darkness? You see things that no one else notices..."

As if a balloon of energy had popped inside him, the man's fire was extinguished. His body slumped and fear starting to make itself known. "Are you for real?" he asked quietly.

"Yes. I have magic. And whether you know how to access it or not, you have magic. You can see Charles, you aren't surprised by my spell—help me to help you."

"Nice one, Jerry McGuire." Charles smirked, then got my elbow in the ribs.

The man stared at me. His gaze flicked to Charles before settling back on me. Softly, almost as if he knew he was damning himself, he said, "Yeah, I seen guys like that before.

They don't usually bother me. Seen a lot of hot ladies walkin' around the place, like you said. Stick to the shadows. I used to point them out to people. I mean, shit, they were right there. No way was I the only one seein' 'em. I used to get pissed, you know? I ain't no liar. I thought it was some joke on the dumb orphan kid. Well fuck that—I got in a few fights over it. But then I got locked in the psyche ward. That changed some shit. I got smart after that. Started playing the man's game. So now, I see one of them big fuckers, I let it be. I mind my own business, and I keep walkin'. Except...you followed me. And you're human. But he's...one of them. Curiosity got the better of me. My bad."

"Have you served time?" I asked. It was a personal thing to ask, but I needed to know the sort of guy I was thinking about taking back to the Mansion. Because I did have to take him back. A fighter with magic? Even if Cato wasn't pushing the uniting of the species, he was still a prize.

He tried to roll his shoulders, but my spell wouldn't let him move freely. "Yeah. Got out of the orphanage and didn't have nowhere to go. Fell in wit' a street crew. I did petty shit at first—stealin' cars and stuff. I did ok so I moved up to the big time. I wasn't runnin' no drugs, though. Packing shit around like a donkey? Dishin' out to kids? C'mon, man. That shit wasn't for me. I got lazy, got pinched, did some time in the clink, and then got out for good behavior. Never went back. Fuck that. I'm good at fixin' cars so I do that. Not as much money, but screw it, you know? My mom didn't sacrifice her life to have me in and out of jail."

"Your mom...sacrificed her life?" I put my hands in my pockets, trying not to look nosey. Charles, staring like he was, wasn't trying at all.

"Yeah. We had a hole-in-the-wall place. Caught fire when I was a kid. Real young. I don't remember too much. She got me out and went back for my cousin. They didn't make it out. That's what they told me at that scum orphanage."

"And you didn't get a foster family?"

A sneer crossed his face for the first time. He spit. "I'm half black, I talked about invisible people, and I was huge for my age. Naw. Best I got was some joint homes, but got kicked out of a few of them before I got smart." He spit again.

"I learned to shut my mouth. I learned really quickly," I admitted, stepping closer. I recognized that lost look in his eyes. The feeling that he'd never been loved. That no one wanted him. Utterly and completely alone.

I'd been lucky enough to find Stefan. Then a father and a weird uncle with a staring problem. And a bunch of guys and gals who had pledged their life to me. I had family now. This guy was still trying to make it on his own. He was trying to deal with some crazy secrets while getting his life on track. It was commendable, and for better or worse, I was totally going to adopt him.

If he didn't try to kill me, at least.

"Your mother was a human?" I asked, already considering letting loose those bands.

"I'd think you were crazy for askin' that shit ten minutes ago." The man chuckled and looked away from me. "Yeah, she was human. Didn't know my dad. Saw a picture of him once. Big, white fucker. He was standing in the shadows, staring at the camera. My mom said she didn't know who he was."

"Then why'd she keep the picture?" Charles was still staring.

"Jesus, Charles, grab some popcorn while you're at it."

"What? This is some entertaining shit. Real life drama."

The man glanced at Charles before turning his focus back to me. "She didn't want to let go of that picture. She had no idea why, neither. Had it framed and everything. Kept it by her bed, but had no idea who it was."

"Then how'd you figure it was your dad?" I asked softly.

He shrugged and went back to staring away from us. "I was young, but always thought my mom being so interested in that picture was weird. It was just in the back of my head, you know. When I got older I tried to confront one of those big fuckers—a chick—I woke up in a park a few days later. Naked with a hard on and no memory. That freaked me out, you know? What the hell, right? I skipped out on a few jobs and just tried to make sense of that shit. Then, one night, it just...came to me. I woke up and I remembered fucking some chick's brains out. Great sex. Kinky shit, too. I was with a few girls at one time. And that picture came back to me. My mom never recovered her memory—or if she did, she didn't say nothing. But maybe there was some feeling there. Maybe some part of her realized where I'd come from. I don't know. I lost her too early to find out."

Charles was right—this was fascinating. I cleared my throat. "Did you...ever seek them out again? Try to confront that chick?"

The man looked at me in disbelief. "Are you for real? And have my memory stolen again? What if I couldn't get it back the next time? Naw, man. I've thought about those chicks, sure. They were hot. And the sex was..." He glanced away from me. "Anyway, I didn't want to risk it. I ain't stupid."

"Ha! She was that stupid! Twice!" Charles pointed at me.

"Can you ever keep your mouth shut?" I berated Charles. I also ignored the man's stare. "Too bad we can't find out if you're right and prove your dad was really one of Charles' kind."

I bit my lip, considering letting him go again.

"Yes there is—I've heard of a few halvsies. It doesn't happen that often, but occasionally..." Charles pushed me aside and stood directly in front of the smaller man. He bent down to be on eye-level. "Human male. I am going to bite your neck right on your vein and suck out some blood. Do not be afraid. There is nothing to worry about."

"What the—"

"Charles!" I batted him away. "Would you stop? Let a pretty girl at the Mansion do it at least. Good God—he doesn't want some guy... Have you lost your mind?"

I faced the man. "Have you ever...like... really wanted something and the unexplainable happened?"

"Sometimes my gun turns a weird shade of red..." the guy admitted in a mumble.

"Awesome. Red will work."

"But it's not great," Charles mediated.

"Charles, he's human. If we teach him how, he can probably get a higher power brewing. I started out red, remember? Quit interrupting." I wished I'd brought Jonas, who was usually quiet and left me to it when he could see that I knew what I was doing. "So, look. I can help you. You aren't a freak or anything. Those guys in the shadows are real. Obviously--there's one standing right next to me. And, you know, you had sex with one. Or many." I cleared my throat again. Finding magical humans had never been this awkward before.

I assessed the spell. "So... You aren't going to do something violent if I release you, right?"

"Try to kill her, human male. I will rock your world." Charles' tattoos lit up.

I blew out a breath. "Taking him into the Mansion is going to suck. With that challenging stare, he's going to have the whole place fighting."

"At least he won't be worried about the orgies, though." Charles smirked.

True.

I stared for a moment, then took a step back. "All right, well... I'm Sasha."

I released the bands.

Nothing happened for a moment. Then the man rolled his shoulders. His arms drifted away from his sides. His gaze, full of wild, raw aggression, drifted to Charles. He flexed.

"I'm your huckleberry. I won't even use magic." Charles' arms rippled with muscle as they lost their color.

The man smirked, then turned his gaze back to me. That fire still burned, but it was subdued now. Under control. "I'm Paulie."

My eyebrows were probably in my hairline. Is that it? I expected him to lose his shit just then. Most of the guys in the Mansion would've.

I nodded with a turned down mouth, my version of asking what was next. "That's Charles. Tomorrow we'll meet the witches. They are human, too, and have access to their magic. Tonight, though, um...we're just going to go back to the Mansion—to the place where guys like Charles live. I'm the Mage there. Do you want to come?"

Paulie started to laugh. He looked up at the sky and shifted so he could look behind him at the mouth of the alley. "I'm going to end up back in the psyche ward. Shadows, mages, witches...what the fuck?"

He let another chuckle out, put his hands on his hips and leaned over. It almost looked like he'd run a mile and was catching his breath. "Screw it." He straightened up. "Yeah, sure. I'll go wit' you and check out all this fairyland bullshit. Why not, right?"

"That's the spirit," I mumbled.

I just hoped he didn't pick a fight with someone and get himself killed.

CHAPTER TWO

*S*till feeling a little awkward, I stupidly motioned Paulie along and set off at a brisk pace back to my car. "Exciting things," I said to myself as we walked. I was trying to convince myself more than actually believing it.

"What are?" Charles asked, walking beside me. Paulie was following along behind. Part of him wasn't sure about going to the Mansion, I could tell. All of this was against everything that had been drilled into him at the mental institution. He'd been shut away from the world for believing this type of thing, after all. But curiosity was probably getting the better of him, like it had me. He wanted to know what really went bump in the night.

He was about to get the crash course.

"Humans with magic. I just love that we can match you fuckers," I said as I turned and kicked out. Charles jumped away before it could land.

"Really, Sasha? If you moved any slower you would've turned to stone."

I threw a punch at Charles' jugular, and another at his stomach. He slapped away the first lazily and let the other land. My fist bounced off a rock hard stomach. A knuckle popped.

"Ow," I muttered, massaging my knuckle.

"When are you going to learn your lesson?" Charles asked with a smile. "You are a human, and therefore weaker—"

I zapped him with a pure shot of fire.

"Ow! Damn it, Sasha!" Charles grabbed his chest where the magic landed and danced away.

"You're stronger physically, but weaker in magic, and a huge boob. Suck on that." I sauntered ahead of him across the street and into another alleyway.

"I asked for a transfer, did I tell you that?" Charles asked, hanging back with Paulie.

"You tell me that every time I best you, idiot. And no you didn't."

"I could've."

"You could've also grown a brain, but I see no evidence..."

"Paulie, bro, don't get on her detail," Charles muttered. "You get the offer and you walk the other way. It's just not worth the aggravation. Plus, you'd have to deal with Jonas, and he is a prickly bastard. If he smiles at you, you just keep walking. Seriously, bro. That's not a place you want to be."

"How old are you?" I heard Paulie ask.

I couldn't help but burst into laughter as I exited the other side of the alley and turned left. I fished in my pocket for keys as my gaze fell on a white BMW. My eyebrows rumpled as I glanced up the block, looking for my Firebird. I turned around and looked at the building, spotting the bright yellow "sweet thang" painted on the wall over other graffiti. I stared back down at the BMW.

"Where's my car..." I glanced around again as Charles stepped up, the confusion I felt crossing his face. I was about to ask if I was losing my mind, and maybe we parked somewhere else, when my phone rang.

Taking it out of my back pocket, I saw "Cato" written across the top. I put it to my ear. "Hello?"

"Sasha?"

"Yes. Hi Cato."

"Oh, Sasha, so lovely to hear your voice. How are you these days? Did you do anything interesting tonight?"

Cato always opened the conversation with pleasantries. He could be under attack and he'd still chat about the color of the flowers on his desk. Being hundreds of years old, time meant nothing to him.

"I found a human that is strong in magic. Uneducated, he is at red level, but I think I can get him higher. He looks mean and a little violent. I just hope he won't provoke fights at the Mansion and get himself killed."

I heard a huff behind me. Paulie didn't think much of that idea. That worried me more.

"Oh fabulous, Sasha. That is great. You know, some people don't follow through with their promises. They tell me they are working on things I deem of the highest importance, but unfortunately their attention wavers."

Because you sound harebrained most of the time. And I'm still not sure I'm doing the right thing. "Uh huh."

"Well, Sasha," Cato continued. An edge crept into his voice. "Human magic workers are essential, as you know. You need to start working with them. Link with them, constantly. Constantly, Sasha. Start with a few people and work some spells. Then spread out into larger and larger circles. Bigger and bigger, do you hear me, Sasha? I want mammoth circles. You will be the pinnacle, and your human magic workers will stretch out below you like a pyramid."

"Okay," I said hesitantly. I couldn't help but hear the fervor in his voice. Just as I had previously worked with his assurance that we needed more magical humans in our ranks, now I was responding to the determination that we should form a huge link. "Why, though, Cato? This sounds..."

"Sasha, above everyone, you've always had faith. Keep that now. The worst may not come to pass, but it may. And because it may, we must be prepared, you and I. You are my secret weapon. I am not the best on my own, Sasha. But together, I think we can be."

I opened my mouth in confusion, but didn't get the chance to question him before he was rattling on.

"Fare you well, Sasha. And keep your eyes open. The Council is weak and the enemy are many."

The phone went dead. I stared down at the bright face, my ocean wave wallpaper now taking up the screen. "The guy is cracked. There are no two ways about it."

"Cato?" Charles asked, striding back toward me with a puzzled expression.

"Yeah. He wants me to get all the humans together and practice forming huge links."

Charles glanced at Paulie, seriousness creeping into Charles' expression. "He thinks trouble's coming. The word at the Council is that Cato gets a sixth sense when trouble is on its way. He sounds like a looney old male, but I'd do what he says."

"I'd planned on it, Charles, I just wished I knew a little more about the whole thing."

Charles cocked his head as he stared down at me. The shadows etched his striking features. "Are you sure?"

The seriousness in his eyes reminded me of the challenges we'd had to endure at the Council. Charles was probably right —perhaps I didn't want to know more. Not yet. Not until I was confronted with it and could do something about it.

"Good call. So, where's my car?" The cool evening was turning into a hard bite of cold that seeped through my sweatshirt and raked my arms. I shivered.

"Well, okay." Charles turned to stare at the wall with his hands braced on his hips. "I remember those words. Remember? I said, 'This spot was made for you, sweet thang.'"

"Hard to forget, Charles."

"So it should be here."

"It musta got boosted. What kind of car was it?" Paulie asked, content to hang out on the sidelines and watch Charles and I scratching our heads.

"It didn't get stolen, bro. That thing was a piece of shit." Charles looked out across the street.

"It was not a piece of shit!" I was lying a little. My poor baby had deep, thick scratches down the body, a plethora of dents, a crack in the windshield, and other defects that only mattered if you cared about appearance. Since I only cared about a car with no car payments, and going fast, I was all set.

Except for now, I was missing a car.

"I'd think this was a joke, but Jonas has no sense of humor." I stared at my phone, wondering if I should call him to ask.

"Ann?" Charles' gaze swung my way.

I shrugged. "Possible, I guess. She even has spare keys. But she'd leave a clue or something. I doubt she'd just take it and leave us stranded."

"Human male." Charles turned his attention to Paulie. "Do you have a car?"

"Naw. Didn't have the cash after going legit." Paulie stared back at Charles. If he was embarrassed by that fact, there was no way to tell. The man had obviously been through the fires and had picked himself up, fixed his life, and moved on. He was a survivor, just like me. I hoped it showed in his magic. Cato would be tickled that there was another human who wouldn't say die.

I hung my head. No sense ignoring the obvious. "Well, it's gone, obviously. I really hope it's a joke and hasn't been towed. That would totally suck." I sighed, staring at that white BMW for one more moment. "Alright, c'mon, let's hoof it. I'm cold and I don't feel like calling Jonas and begging for a ride."

"I'm your huckleberry," Charles retorted, waiting for me to get to his side before crossing the street beside me.

"Would you quit with that line?"

An hour later we were most of the way home and Charles was starting to get jumpy. Movement was good, but without violence of some sort, his attention wandered. He was punching bushes and kicking at pebbles.

He slapped a leaf and then did a low roundhouse kick to a flower. "I feel like Chuck Norris."

"I don't think Chuck Norris got famous for ruining flora."

"Did you know that when Alexander Bell invented the telephone, he had three missed calls from Chuck Norris?"

Paulie barked out a laugh. I couldn't help my own chuckles as we came to a large park with an overgrown baseball diamond, nestled between voluminous trees and high grasses. We were in a poorer district just outside of town and it showed. Potholes marred the street, the uneven sidewalk tried to grab my feet where I walked and the park was in complete disarray. It was a shame that the city spent their money on people that didn't need it as badly as this community. Way of the world.

"Did you call the pound?" Charles tried, looking at the high grasses and wildflowers we were approaching. I had every belief that a few would lose their lives for his entertainment.

"You're not even thinking, anymore. The pound Charles? I don't drive a dog."

"I'd like to ride one." He waggled his eyebrows.

"She's a mountain lion, for the millionth time, and Ann would totally let you if you were nice to her."

"I am nice to her!"

"Constantly asking for sex is not wooing a girl, Charles."

Paulie huffed out a laugh behind us. He'd stayed a few paces back the whole walk, and had been silent most of the time, only once uttering a warning of "Car," when I was about to cross the street. Even though the guy looked all kinds of dangerous, his overall vibe was actually more on the relaxed side. He seemed grounded and patient, content to let life rage around him, comfortable in his skin.

"Oh yeah, human male? What do you know about it?" Charles glanced over his shoulder.

"I know that women are nothing but trouble," Paulie said in his deep rasp.

"I like him," Charles announced.

"Cute." I glanced at the overgrown field to my left as a strange feeling came over me. Something felt like it brushed against my magic, and then weaved within it. But it wasn't like normal magic. It wasn't someone weaving spells or even feeling for other magic workers. It was wholly different. It reminded me of—

I felt a large hand on my shoulder, startled to see Paulie suddenly right beside me, putting his body between the park and me. "There's something out there," he said in a low tone, looking out across the dark field.

"It's a Mata," I clarified. "I can feel its magic. Only one, I think." I pointed at the distant trees beyond the field. Deep pools of shadow lurked between the trees. Crickets had stopped their song, uncomfortable with whatever lay in their midst.

"Probably just on patrol," Charles said.

"He must know it's us, though. We're upwind." I hadn't meant to hush my voice, but my words came out a whisper all the same. Something was not quite right about this. While the Mata were patrolling a lot of the city, I was pretty sure this was our territory.

"What's a Mata?" Paulie said, still blocking me off from the park with his body.

"Shape changers. Were-animals. Were-wolves, were-mountain lions and the like," I answered softly. My gaze scanned the tree trunks. Sometimes a Mata in animal form was in plain sight and you couldn't see it because it stood absolutely still next to a tree.

"Witches, mages and now humans who turn into animals. I feel like I'm losing my mind." Paulie's voice sounded strained.

"You'll get used to it." I felt my body tingle with danger. My magic prickled in the presence of a shifter magic, sensing it moving slowly toward us.

"If that's one of Tim's, he either doesn't know who the hell we are, the smell of my kind, or he's gone feral. There's something not right about this," Charles said, dropping his usual lighthearted manner. His tattoos swirled a light gold. "I feel him coming. He knows we're here, but he's in no hurry to show himself."

"My thoughts exactly. Paulie, get behind me," I said in a low tone as we neared the end of the baseball field. The trees were starting to close in on the rest of the park, the long grasses reaching out into the sidewalk to brush our legs as we passed. "You don't want to get blasted with magic."

Paulie dropped back a little. Charles and I walked a little faster to get in front of him. I felt the movement of magic, coming closer. Nearing us but well hidden somewhere among the trees and long grasses. A bird exploded from a tree some distance to our left, warning us of something approaching.

"Do you see anything Charles?" I asked in a frantic whisper. Slow and purposeful, the Mata stalked us like a predator.

Charles peered into the dark spaces with a bent body and

squinting eyes. He shook his head slowly as he drew his sword. The blade flashed with magic. He took the gun out of his belt and handed it back to Paulie without hesitation.

"I feel the movement, but I can't..." Charles shook his head in jerks, frustration making his brow crinkle.

"Should we take off, do you think?" I asked in a squeak.

"Four legs are faster than two," Paulie said with an edge to his voice. The rasp had deepened into something hinting at unspeakable violence. Neither Charles nor I could help but glance back.

His face held in a placid mask of disinterest, Paulie seemed lost in his own fantasyland. His eyes flashed with wild rage that was kept on a tight leash. I had no doubt that if something charged from the trees; Paulie would rush at it with a burst of strength and speed. He looked like he'd seen horrors in his life, and had obviously never turned tail and ran. I hoped this was no different.

"He's going to fit in just fine," Charles muttered, his gaze sweeping back to the park. "I hate this type of shit. Just show yourself, bro." Charles gave a frustrated huff. "Should we just go in and drag whoever it is back out? Two of us against—"

"Three," Paulie interrupted Charles.

"Two magic workers and one antsy human against a varmint. Let's just go get him."

"This guy seems...so controlled," I said as we neared the edge of the park. Trees pushed almost up to the sidewalk. Shadows of bushes and grasses lay beneath and around them. Branches swept low, disappearing into the darkness. At the tree line stood a fence surrounding someone's unkempt yard. I stopped at the line, staring into the black.

I felt the prickle between my shoulder blades. It was no more than ten feet away. I should have been able to see whatever it was that my magic had located. I even pointed at it, drawing the attention of the others to a low-lying tree branch. But I couldn't make out any other shapes.

"Is it invisible?" Charles asked. His knuckles were white on his sword.

"No. He doesn't have that kind of magic. It's all shifter magic I sense. He's in animal form, but..."

"A rat, maybe," Paulie said in a contemplative tone. "Or a small animal."

My lips turned down in thought as I gave a slight nod. "Could be, I guess. The smallest animal Tim has is a badger, I think. I know him, though. Jacob and he wouldn't be hiding."

"What if it isn't one of Tim's?" Charles shifted impatiently. "Look, Sasha, blast that thing out, let me go get it, or let's move on. Standing here talking about it is embarrassing because you know it can hear us."

He was right. It was close enough to hear everything we said. We were standing in the glow of a street light with a big moon shining down on us—it could clearly see us and it wasn't showing itself. So controlled. Stalking us. But why?

My mind flashed back to Cato's call. Then to Paulie's sudden appearance and all the humans Birdie was finding. Then this trouble in my hometown. Fate wasn't done with me yet.

CHAPTER THREE

"C'mon, let's go," I said with a calm voice. I didn't want this person to know my thought process. Or my alarm.

"We're just going to leave it at that?" Charles asked. "I don't like people trying to sneak up on me. It's irritating."

"Just...c'mon." I gave him a small zap to get him to move.

The park fell away behind us as we passed the fence and quickened our pace. Our spy started to move, but not toward us.

"It's headed back the way it came. Maybe it was just checking us out because it heard us..." I noted.

"Still not one of Tim's, though. Couldn't be," Charles said, glancing back. "Couldn't be. They all know my smell. And everyone—and I mean everyone—knows about you. You're a pack friend. It couldn't be one of his."

"What does that mean?" Paulie asked from behind us.

"It means Tim's got a visitor in his territory, bro, and he's going to lose his shit when he finds out." Charles slapped a bush.

"I doubt Stefan is going to be too thrilled, either." I bit

my lip, thinking about the slow, purposeful movements of the shifter.

"That happen often?" Paulie asked.

"What?" I looked behind me and tried to read his face. He had the same placid expression he'd had all night. The wildness in his eyes had calmed, though. He was back to patient and relaxed.

"Random people threatening you."

"Usually we get to actually confront it." Charles kicked another rock. "I don't like that creeper bullshit. What kind of game do you think that cat was playing?"

"Cat..." I let that word roll around in my mouth. It sounded about right, with the slow stalking and contented waiting. "I bet it was some kind of cat."

"Mountain lion?" Charles asked with a growl.

"No. I know Ann's magic. But cat fits. Hmm."

"So...you guys weren't kidding about the violence. You carry swords and shit, huh?" Paulie tried again.

"No, I wasn't kidding. Yes, we carry sharp objects. And yes, danger often turns into a battle. It used to be that walking through town got you a sword fight and a few demons. These days..." I let my voice trail away as we got closer to home. I wanted to run. I wanted to get to the safety of the Mansion and tell Stefan what had happened. I wanted to hear what he said.

I also needed to call Tim. He'd want to know about a stranger immediately.

"These days we're just waiting for the balloon to pop. The problem now is, we don't know what surprises will be thrown at us." I shoved my hands in my pockets. I had a feeling demons would be the least of my problems.

As we turned onto our home block a half hour later, my feet protesting loudly, I stopped dead. My car sat right out in front of the Mansion. A white piece of paper waved at me in the breeze from beneath my windshield wiper. The windows were all up and in place, no new dents or scratches marred the sides as far as I could see. When we drew closer I saw that nothing was out of place inside.

Maybe Jonas had played a prank. Maybe Charles' humor was rubbing off...

I curled my fingers under the cold metal of the door handle and tugged. Locked. I glanced up as Charles tried the other side. Also locked.

"Someone stole my car, brought it home for me, and then locked up?" I asked, snatching the note off the windshield.

"Someone's messing with you," Paulie observed from the grass, taking turns in staring at the car and then the huge Mansion. "I've lived in this town most my life. Ain't never seen nothing like this. Looks like it's from the turn of the century. And here it is, squatting here. Been here this whole time, I got no doubt. I'm losing my mind."

Ignoring Paulie, I opened the letter and read the contents.

HOPE YOU DON'T MIND. JUST CHECKING YOU OUT.

A SHIVER RACED UP MY BACK. THERE WAS NO SIGNATURE.

I gestured Charles over as I unlocked and opened the car door. "Stick your nose in there. What do you smell?"

"What the fuck took you so long, human?" Jonas' voice called across the expanse of grass in front of the Mansion.

"Super. He's in a colorful mood." I got out of the way of Charles, not bothering to look over at Jonas until I heard, "What the fuck are you staring at?"

I spun and threw up a barrier between Jonas and Paulie while Charles stuck his face into my car. He slid inside and looked all around, sniffing the air.

Jonas stood at the barrier, eyes on fire, staring directly at Paulie. Paulie stood as calm as could be, but that wildness burned in his gaze as he stared right back at Jonas. The man had no fear. Equally as clear, Jonas wanted to fix that.

"Jonas, we've had a really long night. Can you just give him a break for a moment? He doesn't know your customs." I squeezed the bridge of my nose. It never helped, but it gave me something to do.

"Why the hell is he eye-ballin' me?" Jonas growled.

I sighed and leaned against the car as Charles got out. He shut the door and glanced between Jonas and Paulie with unfocused eyes. He turned to me with a rumpled brow. "Shifter. Definitely. But I've never smelled that odor before, so either he isn't one of Tim's, or I've never met him. It's a pretty strong magical smell." Charles shifted, his eyes utterly serious. "Tim strong. Like...alpha strong."

Jonas' head turned our way.

"So what does that mean?" I asked quietly.

"You saw how the Boss behaved with Dominicous in his space. Alphas do not like other alphas in their space unless the hierarchy is clearly defined and accepted. The Boss and Dominicous—that was defined, but not really accepted by the Boss. So...fireworks. This guy...he's probably a stranger. And he's got some powerful magic. Tim's going to lose his shit." Charles mimed an explosion.

"You going to fill me in?" Jonas finally asked. Paulie went back to staring at the Mansion. I let the magic drift away back into the world.

"Why is he sizing me up, though?" I asked with a shaky voice. "What do I have to do with anything?"

"He's learnin' how this town works," Paulie said. "That's what we did when I ran in that street gang. You don't just go into a new territory and take what you want. That'd get you dead. Naw, man, you go in, figure out who's in charge, figure out if you can dominate, and then take over. If you can't dominate right off, you got to figure out if it's worth taking them out and claiming the spot. If you got someone more organized than you, with more fire power—well, you back the hell out, you know? You don't play that game. Someone weak? Or someone you can work with? Cool. Got yourself a wider area."

"Human, what is going on," Jonas barked.

If Paulie decided to hang around, Jonas would have to learn our names or it would get pretty confusing.

"Charles, fill him in. I'm going to go call Tim and see Stefan. Paulie, come with me. I want to know your heritage, and you need a blood test for that." I started toward the Mansion, promising safety and comfort. And Stefan, my love. As I walked I could feel him, tugging at my middle, beckoning me closer.

"I ain't giving no blood sample," Paulie said as he started forward with me. "I'll check out this scene, like I said, but there ain't no way I'm lettin' some doctor at my vein."

"It won't be a doctor," I said. "And trust me, you won't be complaining. What's your type? Slim and willowy or strong and well built? Or both—you can have more than one."

I stepped up onto the porch so my eye level would be even with Paulie and turned around abruptly. He stopped and looked at me in mild surprise. I pinned him with a serious gaze. "Do not stare at anyone in here, okay? You are a human. Those inside might see an alpha in you, but you are still human—they'll challenge for the sake of their pride. You won't get three feet without a fight. Win that one, and you won't get three more without another one. I'm content to let you fight your way through here any other time, because you seem smart enough not to get yourself killed, but tonight I've got shit to do, okay? So as a favor to me, just keep your eyes down. If you don't plan on doing me any favors, I will wrap your ass up in magic and drag you down the hall. Got me?"

Humor danced in Paulie's eyes. A smile tickled his lips. "You."

"What?"

"You're my type."

Charles barked out laughter. "Don't advertise that, bro. After you meet the Boss, you'll know why."

"Strong-willed female not afraid to take command," Jonas stated, waiting for us to go through the door. "Good taste. Shows he'll follow orders if given by someone dominant enough. Shows he doesn't care if that dominance is by a male or female, as long as the leadership is sound. If he can hold his magic better than his dick, he'll fit in. As long as I don't kill him first."

"That last part just had to be said, huh Jonas?" I said with an eye roll. I glanced at Charles. "What woman do you recommend?"

"Already on it," Charles said, tapping a text into his phone. He stared for a minute, his phone lighting up his face. "She's smooth as silk. And she likes to cuddle, so he'll have a place to sleep after."

"You running a whore house?" Paulie said in disgust. "I don't pay for—"

"You'll see," I said, waving him away. "These people are insane when it comes to sex."

"You said you got your memory back last time, bro. You should already know what you're stepping into." Charles' phone vibrated. He glanced up at me and winked. "All set. She knows he's human. Doesn't care."

I nodded and turned toward the door. Only steps inside I saw Selene, the woman Charles must've called. Slim but muscular, she wore a corset and a thong with a see-through, red chemise swirling down her body and around her thighs. A face that would make cupid weep with heart-shaped, pouty lips and large, luminous eyes burning with fire and arousal. I had woman-wood for this girl. It was hard not to. She was as gorgeous as they come and more. She was a fearless fighter, high up in the Watch, down to earth, and cool to hang around with. It was hard to be jealous of her rock-star personality, but I kind of wanted to trip the bitch because she was so damn pretty.

"You're in good hands, Paulie," I said with a smirk, and stepped out of the way.

I watched as Paulie's earlier disgust turned into burning lust as he took in what was in front of him. His mouth dropped open and his body went rigid. And then it hit me. Like a wood stove on a cold, winter's day, the smell wafted around my head pleasantly.

"He does that smelly arousal thing!" I exclaimed, pointing at Paulie. I beamed at Charles. "Guys can do it, too! What did that mean again? Fortuneteller blood, or whatever, right? Oh my God, so cool. I totally win for finding a human magic worker!"

"Hmmm," Selene purred as she got closer, all hip and boob, obviously smelling what I did. "What a treat. And not like the typical, weak human. You'll do nicely." She ran a manicured hand up Paulie's chest and smiled into his awe-struck face.

"We need to know if he's halvsies," Charles said.

"And I get to take blood? Ohuuu, lovely." Selene ran another hand up Paulie's chest and hooked her arms around his neck. Almost as tall as him, she rose on her toes, leaned in and nibbled his lips while she pressed her body against his. His hands came around and rested at the small of her back. She swirled her hips in a circle, pressing firmly against him in slow gyrations. She wasn't waiting—she planned to get started right then and there.

His hands shaking, Paulie drew her in harder before sliding his hold down to clutch her muscular butt. In a rapid loss of control, he deepened their kiss, opening her mouth with his in a deep, sensuous kiss. One hand slid over her round buttock and down between her cheeks, running his fingers against her gyrating sex.

"Good God, he'll fit in just fine," I said, breathless. My sexy systems raged to life as I stood, like a voyeur. I needed Stefan. I needed to be a participant.

"Thanks, Charles," Selene purred as she ran her thigh up the outside of Paulie's leg and hooked it around his hip.

Paulie used the increased access to his advantage. He dipped his fingers into the seam of her thong and felt up between her sex. One finger dipped into her body.

"Mmm, that's right." Selene's head fell back and she worked her hips in time with the plunging of his finger.

"Oh holy moly," I heard myself say. I was walking the next moment.

I didn't think to call Tim. Or say goodbye to the guys. Or notice the people saying "Mage." Or anything, really. I felt Stefan's pull, and I felt my need. That was it.

I found my way up to our wing and burst into the room. The lights were turned down low and the shades were up, displaying the blanket of stars until they reached the horizon. Not a moment to lose, I followed that pull to the dining room where flames of two candles danced on a table set for two. Stefan waited at the head of the table, the blood link colored with an answering hunger. He felt my lust and was responding with his own.

He stood as I came into sight, his muscular body covered in expensive slacks and a button-down shirt that hugged his delicious body just right. He took a step toward me as I closed the three steps to him. I met him in a rush, climbing up his body and wrapping my legs around his middle. His hard bulge rubbed against my aching sex. His lips met mine, needy and passionate. I opened to him, delighted to be filled with his taste, wine and spice.

He spun me around and cleared his side of the table with a sweep of his arm. Crystal and china clinked or crashed to the side. A candle fell over, the wax dousing the flame. My butt hit the table a moment before my back did. I squeezed my legs, pulling his body in tighter, gyrating against that large bulge.

Stefan's hand slid in between our bodies to tug at the buttons on my jeans. I loosened my hold so he could strip me from the waist down, and then pull his slacks out of the way. His large manhood sprang free, the velvety skin hitting off my warm wetness. My eyes fluttered and I turned into liquid as his shaft rubbed along my slipperiness. I moaned, clutching his shoulders, losing myself in his kiss. In the feel of him.

He backed off so he could strip my upper half. As the chilled air assaulted me, my nipples contracted. He bent, teasing one with his tongue, and then the other, before sucking it in. I moaned as he increased the suction to something bordering on exquisite pain. Slowly, as his mouth and fingers worked my nipples, pleasure and pain mingling together, his blunt head pushed into me. Spikes of pleasure burst through my body, arching me up to his mouth. Savoring the feel of him sliding into my body.

"Yes, Stefan," I exalted.

His mouth trailed up my chest and to my neck. The sharp pain of teeth offset the exquisite pleasure of his manhood pushing all the way inside me. The draw of his mouth connected with the sensations of his hard length working. Without warning, a blast of orgasm stole my breath and rocked my body. I shivered beneath him; my body so hot it felt like it was burning up.

He took another slow draw as he penetrated me. My body

immediately went back on the edge. Begging for more. Ready for another release.

He stood up, his hips against mine. He ripped off his shirt and stared down at me, letting me marvel at his perfectly sculpted body. His hips thrust forward and back. He grabbed my ankles and pulled them so my legs were against his chest. He pumped harder into me. Filling me in plunges. Hitting off my insides just right.

My body flashed hotter. Hotter still. Sweat broke out along my body. His, too. He glistened as he worked, his cut muscles perfect.

"Yes, Stefan," I uttered, watching his perfect form.

He pushed harder as he dropped his hand between my legs and played. I sucked in a breath. My eyes rolled back in my head. I squeezed my eyes shut, focused on the pleasant violation. Feeling him deep inside me. My panting filled the room. My moans replaced those.

"I'm...I'm...I—" My eyes fluttered as I shivered again, harder this time. I felt Stefan quake over me in completion. He lowered his body between my legs and braced his elbows on the table.

His lips softly touched mine. "I like what this Mansion does to you."

I couldn't help but smile. "I like that you don't mind when I ruin your dinner to get laid."

"You didn't ruin anything. You just brought your own hors d'oeuvres."

I smiled into his lips. "Now that that's off my chest, I have some things to tell you about tonight."

CHAPTER FOUR

$\mathcal{I}$ got out of bed with my hair looking like a windstorm in progress. I was also completely naked, hunched, and not in the mood for chatter. Why? Because it was the middle of the day, four hours after I'd gone to bed, and I had to meet the witches for their club thing.

I really wished I hadn't said I'd do it. Although, at the time, I hadn't realized I was being stalked by some strange shape changer who was not afraid to steal my car and make me walk home.

After Stefan had sexed me up, I'd gone over all the events of the night before. When I got to the person hiding in the darkness, a lethal edge crept into his eyes, made worse when I told him what the note had said. He listened to Charles' findings before pulling out his phone. It was dawn by then, but Tim had answered anyway.

"Stefan," Tim said. The two never said hi to each other. They trusted each other, and would work together, but they wouldn't consent to being overly civil about it.

Men were dumb.

"Are you aware of a fellow alpha in your territory?" Stefan

asked in a matter-of-fact way.

Silence reigned. If the counter on the phone call wasn't running, I would've thought he had hung up. After a few moments, Tim said, "What was that?"

Charles had been right. Tim didn't like another alpha in his territory any more than Stefan did. This one was a stranger, too. And lurking. That had to be so much worse.

I explained the events of the night to Tim just as I had to Stefan, but focusing on the shifter elements. Tim waited until I was finished, not doing so much as clearing his throat while I talked. After I'd fallen silent, he said, "You think it was a cat, then?"

"I don't know, but that fits, doesn't it? Creeping around, silent, stalking, waiting and watching..."

"You're sure it was a shifter who took your car?"

"Charles is. I am, personally, sure it was a shifter in that park. One I didn't recognize."

"And the scent—Charles said he didn't recognize it, either?" Tim had confirmed.

"Right."

The line fell silent again. After another minute, he said, "Did he tamper with your car? Break in?"

"Not at all. It was locked when I left it, and locked when I found it. He must've used a key to start it."

"And you have your keys."

"Yeah. That's how I opened the door."

"Who else has keys?" Tim asked.

"I have a spare set in the key bowl, and they are still there, and Ann has a set. There is no way a shifter would've made it up a set of stairs without me or one of Stefan's kind noticing."

"Why does Ann have a set?" Tim asked.

I hesitated and looked at Stefan. Ann used my car when Tim had ordered her to stay put and had people monitoring the comings and goings of vehicles. She would still sneak out if she could, and do whatever she felt like doing with my wheels. I didn't really want to blow her cover. "Just in case I lose mine. She runs fast."

Tim let the silence reign again, hopefully not dissecting the omitted truth, before asking, "Does she still have those keys?"

It was a good question. One I should've thought of. "Um... I don't know."

"Hold on." Tim was gone for a few minutes, apparently not taking his phone with him. When he came back, he said simply, "They're gone."

A shiver ran up my spine. "What do you mean they're gone? Did she lose them? Did she give them to someone?"

"I woke her up to ask. She said she hasn't used your car since visiting you directly after the Council—when everyone was healing. She put the keys in her basket, and now they were gone. She remembers a strange smell in her room yesterday but figured it was someone new that had wandered into the wrong room. I don't blame her for not looking into it further."

"That didn't need to be said." I stared at Stefan who calmly stared back. "How would anyone have known those were mine?"

"He had to have been in the area for a while," Stefan answered with an even voice. It was a dangerous voice, one prone to extreme acts of violence. One that would rip Tim's command out from under him if I were in trouble in any way.

It wasn't a healthy component to their new working relationship.

Tim must've heard it because he said, "He's doing his homework, Stefan. But he didn't realize we had someone of Sasha's level, that's obvious. I might've followed you and watched, like he did, if I wanted to learn more about you. You might sense me, but you wouldn't know exactly who I was.

But Sasha's magic has a greater reach—something I learned at the Council facility and at the battle. She is way above the others in your clan, Stefan. This guy obviously doesn't know that. Or at least he didn't. I bet he does now. Did he mess up, or is this what he was trying to achieve? And whom is he working for? My shifters wouldn't care about advanced magic, or know anything about it, if it wasn't for you guys and Sasha. If this was his plan, he is reporting to someone. Someone of your kind, Stefan, I'd bet."

"His next movements will determine the kind of man we're dealing with," Stefan said. "And his motives."

"He is a shifter so I will deal with this, Stefan." A hard edge had crept into Tim's voice.

Stefan had leaned forward over the phone, his substantial muscles flexing dangerously. He'd rolled his neck and willed control. "For now. But if my mate is threatened or followed one more time, I will find this man and kill him if she or one of her guards don't do it first. I will not be waiting for you and yours to play dominance games, is that clear?"

Silence had descended for a time before Tim said, "Understood. I can't fault you—I'd do the same thing. Otherwise, leave this to me. I'll need to work your territory, though. I need access to the whole area."

"Done. My people will turn a blind eye." Stefan had straightened up a fraction before saying, "If you need backup, you got it. If he tries to kill you and take over, or succeeds, I'll probably kill him. I've resigned myself to you—I will not roll over and play nice with a stranger who hasn't fought beside me. Plan for that eventuality."

Again there was a pause. "Noted."

The line had gone dead. The fact that Tim hadn't argued was the same as saying, "Thanks." These guys were idiots with each other, but at least they spoke the same language.

"So you don't think I was really the target?" I asked

Stefan.

"No, love. I think Tim was right—this shifter was doing his homework. He's able to get in, and out of, Tim's compound undetected, which means stealth. It also means he's scouted that place heavily. Instead of acting, or challenging Tim for the throne, he starts to scout my people. Takes notes. He's not afraid to let us know he's in the area, either, which I find strange. His tactics are strange. Unless he wanted to observe away from here and thinks he's too elusive to be found... That's a possibility if the shifter is dense."

I shook my head. Too many possibilities. I was no good at this kind of stuff.

And it had been so quiet the last few weeks without Andris.

I shrugged off the memory of the night before as I trudged toward the bathroom.

"Do you want me to get up?" Stefan asked from a heap on the other side of the bed.

"Why? So you can be miserable with me?"

He grunted and rolled over. Once everything had been made official on the mate front, Stefan had turned into a huge softy where it concerned me. He'd bring me breakfast in bed, leave meetings half way through to walk me down the hall, and touched me constantly, regardless of who saw. Charles called it the honeymoon period. Whatever it was, I loved it.

Except when I was cranky and tired.

I took a shower barely half awake then stared at myself in front of the mirror. A red-eyed monster stared back.

After I brushed my teeth, combed my hair, and dressed, I caught sight of my reflection once more and pondered makeup. The red-eyed monster grimaced.

The witches could see me ugly. It wouldn't be the first time.

It was only after I reached into the medicine cabinet for

some mouthwash, that a nagging fear shot through me. It was the Sunday after the week of sugar pills—I needed to start a new pack of pills at bedtime. A shot of panic raced through me—I did have another package, right? I wasn't out yet? I knew I needed to visit the doctor soon to renew the prescription, but I was pretty sure I had a month left.

Lord help me if I didn't—there was no way Stefan would use protection if there was a chance we could get pregnant. I could deny him sex but he was a cunning bastard. He'd woo me and beguile me and then wink at me and I'd roll over and spread my legs. The man was too hot for his own good. It was almost a problem.

I yanked a drawer open and rooted through my birth control pouch. There, waiting for me with a smile, was the last package. Oh thank God! I needed to get into the doctor this month, though. I had to get that end of things locked down. I had more than enough time in my life to get pregnant and go visit that weird pregnancy farm these people had. Stefan could wait.

Humming a tune to myself, which sounded like a bee buzzing in flight even to me, I snatched my satchel off the couch, and headed off to the front door of the Mansion. I'd decided to test my bodyguards' reaction time to me leaving without alerting them first. I knew that they got updates on my movements, but they hadn't really been tested yet. I'd hate them to get complacent.

Tee hee!

"Good afternoon, Mage," Timmy, the guy hanging out in the front guarding the entrance, greeted me. He was a human with a tiny flare of magic that Birdie had met in her magical club. Timmy usually reached purple and occasionally, with my help, could reach green. That was mostly useless, as far as spell-working went, but great for when I needed to link for energy for a spell. He got the "front desk" duty firstly because he was human, and staying awake in daytime was a natural thing, and secondly, because humans and Mata stopped by the Mansion at all hours, and the Watch worried someone would notice people disappearing into thin air. That would bring the lookey-loos and self-guided tours. Timmy was in position to stop that.

I wasn't fooled, of course. Timmy was there to keep an eye on my comings and goings. I'd left one time for a quick run to get fast food and suddenly I was no longer trusted.

"Hi, Timmy. Slow day?"

"Always is. But it pays okay and I get to read, so I don't mind. Where ya headed?"

"Oh, just heading out for a walk."

"Uh huh. Okay, see ya."

I gave him a wave and lifted my phone in front of me as I passed, pretending to be enthralled with what was on it. Instead, I watched in the reflection as Timmy eyed me, and then brought up his own phone to make a call.

As I stepped outside I heard, "Yes, sir. The chicken is leaving the coop, sir. S-sorry, no sir, I don't think it's funny to wake you up talking about chickens. I meant Sasha is—"

I didn't wait around for the rest of the conversation. Instead, I sprinted out the door and to my car. No time to lose, I ripped my door open and jammed my key in the ignition. I pulled out into the street with a still silent Mansion behind me and gassed it.

It belatedly occurred to me that I should've been more cautious about getting into my car. With keys missing, anything could've been waiting in there. My bad.

The wind rushed through the open window and licked my face. The chill of the air bit me as I reveled in the glorious fiery oranges and reds of the trees. I took a deep breath and let the steady hum of the motor lull me into a comfortable daze. Not strictly safe while driving, maybe, but without

Charles constantly chattering in my ear, or Jonas grunting and lecturing, I felt free in a way I hadn't in a long time.

A ten-minute drive had me arriving at a busy coffee shop on the outskirts of town. I parked in the lot in the back behind a giant truck so I couldn't be seen from the road, and found Birdie and Delilah sipping coffee outside in the sunshine.

"Hi ladies," I said as I walked up with a bounce in my step.

"Where's your entourage?" Birdie asked, frowning at me. She was an aged woman with a large stature and larger voice.

"Delayed."

"Huh. Look what Delilah went and did!" Birdie exclaimed as she plucked at Delilah's sleeve.

Rolling her eyes, the younger woman lifted her sweatshirt to reveal a circle of runes around her forearm. The other arm had different symbols in the same location. For a tiny woman with large glasses, this was definitely a little out of character.

"It looks okay," I hedged.

"I told her to get some runes that increased working with power. What does she need with throwing when she doesn't have much to throw? No. That was definitely the wrong set for the first time. I chose these—" Birdie lifted the arm of her sweater to reveal a string of angry characters that ran up the loose skin on her forearm until it wrapped around her flabby upper arm.

"Whoa, nice ink grandma," a guy with a Mohawk and a spiked dog collar said as he rolled by on his skateboard.

"Riiigggght. Yeah. Hey, let's go inside. I ditched my body-guards and want to see how long before they find me." I waved them into the warm coffee shop.

I didn't mention that I also wanted to be in a place where I couldn't be watched easily. If that shifter walked in the coffee shop, I'd know. But hanging out somewhere outside with a pair of binoculars or something, I wouldn't recognize the magic. Not from a distance, and not without concentrating.

"Oh, Sasha, aren't they going to be mad?" Delilah asked in a whisper, glancing down the near empty street.

"Oh yeah. Really mad. That'll teach them to spy. My goal is to get home and back in bed before they catch me. Then they'll bust in and piss off Stefan. Payback."

"You're playing with fire, girl!" Birdie followed me into the shop and sat at a cozy seat next to the window. She was kind of missing the point.

"Do you anticipate anyone of interest being at the meeting today? Anyone new?" I asked as I sat down a moment later with a Frappuccino.

"We have a few prospectives." Birdie sipped her coffee. "Not strong, but they are trying. I think we should switch gears and aim for finding breeders, though."

I coughed into my coffee. "What?"

"I've been thinking." Birdie hit me with that focused glare. "Children believe in magic. We feed them the tooth fairy and Santa Claus and the Easter Bunny—but as they realize each of those isn't real, their belief in magic as a whole dries up."

"True..."

"Right. So then, as adults, re-teaching them that magic does exist is tough. There are exceptions, like us, but mostly, it is a tough road. I think we need to start with children. Like the Boss' people do. So, I'm thinking that instead of looking for magic users, we should look for open-minded people who wouldn't mind mixing with Stefan's people."

"You're trying to breed humans..." I summarized with wide-eyes.

"Well?" Delilah defended. "It makes sense, doesn't it?"

"You're in this, too, Delilah?" I couldn't help the incredulous tone.

She raised her chin. "I helped think of it. Besides, Stefan's people—your people, sorry—are excellent lovers. And great boyfriends if you don't mind them screwing around. Any woman would be lucky to—"

"Wait," I held up my hand to stop her. "Don't tell me you're taking part in your own breeding experiment."

"Actually, at first it was more of a 'when in Rome' mentality, but yes. I want to see if we're right. And I'm ready for a baby. Did you know they have a daycare setup? It's free."

I stared at the reserved woman sitting in front of me sipping her coffee with her pinky sticking up and couldn't find any words. She was admitting to not only sexing her way through the Mansion, but to now seeing if that would produce a baby.

"And you said they were great boyfriends?" I asked with a slack jaw. "You know from experience?"

"Fine looking man," Birdie commented.

My mouth opened wider. Birdie had made that comment. The woman who had told someone to stop masturbating or they'd go blind.

"He treats me better than I've ever been treated," Delilah said. "If I get with child, he wants first dibs to mate me and take care of us. And I'm all for it. I really like him."

"First dibs to mate you. Ahm. So...that's like marriage. You know that, right?" I pushed. "I mean, not like human marriage, since you'd both, apparently, still screw around, but he'd become your baby-daddy."

She broke out in a smile this time, excitement sparkling in her eyes.

World. Blown.

I didn't really know what to say. This was weirder than first learning what went on at the Mansion.

"Any luck?" I asked in a wispy voice.

Delilah's face fell. She took a bite of her cookie. "No. Just got a visit from Aunt Flow this morning. Speaking of, do you have any spare...you know? I'm on my last one and we have to go to Birdie's club after this."

"You can say it. Pad. I may not need them anymore, but it's not like I'm Charles!" Birdie glared at Delilah. "And it's our club. You helped found it."

I reached into my handbag and felt around the bottom before I stilled. My world screeched to a halt. My heart started pounding and my head got light. I'd used the sugar pills, which meant I should've had my period. I usually had it a week before Delilah.

This had not dawned on me earlier.

I hadn't had it.

Oh shit!

"I gotta go," I said in a panicked rush.

"What? Why? Is Charles here?" Birdie peered out the window. "I don't see—"

I was already in flight when the knowing look came over Delilah's face. I sprinted outside. I needed time to myself. I needed to think about this.

I needed to get tested!

Holy shit, what if I was pregnant? Oh holy shit!

How did I get pregnant? I was on the pill for Christ's sake. I'd missed a day or two at the Council, but I'd doubled up the next day. That should've worked. I didn't think I'd missed one completely.

I fell into my car. "I didn't miss one," I yelled at my car. "I had an empty pack except for the sugar pills. I can't be pregnant."

I filled my lungs and stilled again.

Remember what is going on in the world around me. This is no time to lose my shit.

Taking another deep breath, I checked the back seat; kind

of hoping a crazy shifter was in it, because he would meet his maker really quickly. Unfortunately, it was empty, leaving me to my problems. Great.

Then I stared straight ahead for a second. I wasn't pregnant. There was no way. Stefan's people had a hard time procreating. Even if the pill didn't hold up, which was 99.9 per cent unlikely, his sperm should've failed. That was the whole deal with his race.

Right?!

Willing calm, I drove to the store like an old lady in rush hour. I didn't want to freak out and run someone over. That would not help the situation. I made it to the closest grocery store and got out on wooden legs. Feeling imaginary things in my stomach, I walked with a zombie lurch toward the feminine aisle. I passed the female hygiene products I really should've had to use last week and came upon the pregnancy tests. Then hesitated.

There was a plethora of options with different prices. Some boasted of super sensitivity and some boasted baby pictures. There were ones with lines, pinks and blues...

"I just want a normal test," I muttered with dismay.

I chose one in the middle price bracket and studied it. The wrapping crinkled as I handled the package. Two lines for yes. One for no. Two tests in the packet.

My heart beating rapidly, I walked toward the checkout with an embarrassment I hadn't felt in a long time. It was like buying condoms for the first time. Or handing a box of tampons to a male clerk. I almost wanted to hold my ring up signifying that I did, in fact, have someone regular that helped me make this potential baby.

I slid the package over the counter with a red face. The fuzzy haired woman in her fifties lazily scanned the barcode of the test, hit a button on her cash register, and glanced at me. "$18.63."

I drew a crumpled twenty out of my wallet and handed it over, brushing a stray piece of hair out of my face. Once I had the change, I waited with forced nonchalance as she slipped my immediate future into a crisp, brown paper bag. Muttering a "thank you," I gingerly picked up the bag like it might be a poisonous snake and walked on eggshells out to my car. I paused beside my door and took a deep breath, watching as the sun floated toward the horizon.

Stefan would still be in bed. If I went home right now, he'd wonder what I was doing home so quickly and he'd get up to check on me. If he found me in the bathroom peeing on a plastic wand, there'd be questions.

I did not want questions until I had answers.

So then what? Hit the park, squat in some bushes and have a pee? Yeah, that'd go over really well. I'd probably get found out by some little kid who would then have very unladylike behavior burned into his head. He'd probably live the rest of his life peering in bushes, terrified of what he might find. Either that, or I'd run into that shifter again while in a very awkward situation.

Excuse me scary stalker man, let me just pull up my pants and put away this pregnancy test and then I will gladly rock your world with magic.

No. Terrible idea.

Like a shotgun blast, the solution came to me—the secret house! I would go to the small bungalow where I'd first lived out my days at the Mansion. The only person who would think to look for me there was Stefan, and only then if there was something the matter. Since I had already muffled the link, and he was asleep, he'd be clueless unless Charles or Jonas told on me. Since Charles and Jonas would both get beat up if that was the case. They wouldn't say a word.

I didn't drive like an old lady this time. I drove like a teenage boy. I took corners like my car was a year old and my tires were newer still. I pulled into the lot at the Mansion, gave a glance around, saw someone standing near the lot's entrance notice me, and put him in a magical cage. He saw me come in, but he wouldn't know where I went after I turned the corner.

As it was still daylight though the sun was starting to sink in the sky, no one else was outside. I slipped beyond the concealment charm of the little bungalow and unraveled the cage to free the guy. I dropped my stuff in the middle of the floor and took the test into the bathroom. Then, remembering there were two tests, I figured I'd better be safe and take them both. I gulped down two glasses of water. It was always better to have a second opinion.

"Okay." I took a deep breath, closed the bathroom door with a soft click, and stared at the package. Slowly, as if defusing a bomb, I took the first test out of the box, tore the wrapping, and stared at it. One white little strip of plastic stared back at me.

I couldn't help but wonder what Stefan would say if I was pregnant. He'd probably be happy. But there were the warnings from Cato, and that crazy Mata stalker. Stefan would go way overprotective...

This isn't helping.

I walked with cement feet to the toilet and did my business. I didn't bother getting up when I'd finished. I sat there, hunched, test held out, watching as the liquid crawled up the test area and ducked inside the plastic. A moment later the liquid was dampening the material within the viewing screen. Slowly, a red line started to form. The picture on the test said two lines meant I was pregnant.

The liquid continued to crawl. Like a turtle in a storm walking up hill, the material slowly, ever so slowly, dampened. A shadow of another pink line started to form.

"There's no way," I said softly.

The first line was deep red at this point, but the second line was a ghost. So light I had to look away and look back, adjusting my eyes. Trying not to stare. Trying not to focus too hard.

The very light pink turned a shade darker.

"Does it count if it's way lighter than the other one?" I muttered. It felt good hearing a voice, even if it was mine. I didn't feel quite so alone.

I should've called Ann for this. I needed someone to hold my hand.

I got up, with my pants around my ankles, and waddled to my purse. I fished out my phone and called Ann.

"Sleeping," came a grumpy voice on the other end.

"I need you," I said in a panic. "Please come to the Mansion."

"What? Why?" Suddenly the sleep cleared from her voice. "What's happened? Are you okay? Where are you?"

"I'm...I don't know. Just come to the Mansion, please. Secret house. Don't tell Tim. Call me when you get here."

"I'll be right there. I'll have to sneak out, though, so have some clothes for me. I'll be in animal form."

"'Kay. Bye." I dropped the phone back to my handbag and picked the test back up for a second viewing.

The second line was decidedly darker. There were two lines.

I didn't know how to feel. I wasn't ready for this. I...

I shook my head. My heart started pounding. I'd barely earned my place, and my mate, and my new life—I was just starting to get used to all the changes, and now this.

I needed another deep breath. And a second opinion.

I waddled back into the bathroom and summoned up another trickle of test material. It was probably heavily diluted with the large amount of water I'd drank, but...well...

I still didn't know how to feel.

The liquid climbed up slower this time. The wait was excruciating.

The first red line flared into existence. And then I noticed something. On the test, pregnant showed the two lines, but the not-pregnant result, with only one line, matched up with the second line on the pregnant result. In other words, it was the second line that was the control line—the line that would come up regardless. The first line was the actual test line.

And that line was really, really red.

Oh, shit. I'm pregnant.

"How did this happen?" I asked the test. "How?"

I looked at the box. It confirmed that two lines, even if one was faint, meant a positive test. And that test was really, really red. Pregnancy red.

I was going to have a baby.

Before I could react a loud crash announced someone coming through the front door in a temper. A moment later, a face covered with rage loomed in the still open bathroom doorway.

"Jesus, Jonas, that face would kill newborn puppies," I said as I dropped the test to the other side of the toilet and out of view. "How about a little privacy, huh?"

"Where the fuck were you, human?" Jonas demanded, stepping into the bathroom. Apparently people on the toilet did not embarrass him as much as it did me.

The front door crashed a second time. "She in here?" I heard Charles yell. "Oh yeah, here's her purse."

Charles' face loomed behind Jonas'. "What the fuck, Sasha? I had to enact the phone tree with the Mata. Why the hell have you been playing speed racer all over this city? Are you trying to get me killed?"

"Why didn't you tell us the meeting was this afternoon instead of this evening?" Jonas demanded in a deep, anger-filled voice. "You left yourself vulnerable."

"Can we talk about this after I get off the toilet, please? This is kind of awkward..." I let my eyebrows reach my hairline as I huffed. Attitude and embarrassment sometimes dislodged Jonas' scrutiny.

As hoped, his gaze took in my precarious position. He took a step back and glared at Charles to get out of the bathroom so he could, too.

My stomach swarmed with butterflies.

Charles was staring in confusion at the box that'd held the pregnancy tests. He slowly, as if finding a piece of gold and unsure if it was real, picked up the white plastic test and inspected it.

"Get out!" I yelled. I needed to hash this out with Ann. I didn't need all my uncertainty known by the male population. That just wasn't how these things were done.

"Is this what I think it is?" Charles asked in a wispy voice I'd never heard before. It was filled with pride, hope, and wonder. It was as if he was looking at a unicorn. He tapped Jonas on the shoulder.

"Charles, seriously, get out!" I yelled frantically.

Everything turned to slow motion. Jonas' shoulders swiveled toward Charles. Both of their gazes fell to the little white wand in Charles' hand.

Charles picked up the box. Jonas took it from him with a delicate, gentle grip. Their gazes went to the directions. Then back to the results. As if synchronized, both heads turned toward me. Their faces were blank. Completely unreadable.

I felt heat soak into my face, but not because I was sitting on the toilet with my pants around my ankles. Suddenly I felt more vulnerable, more exposed, than I ever had in my whole life.

"I didn't mean to," I said overcome by an irrational need to defend myself. "I didn't plan it. I don't know how it happened..."

Both of the guys stared at me.

I felt my eyes sting in fear and uncertainty. "Is Stefan going to be mad? The timing is bad, I know, but it's an accident. I promise." My voice sounded so tiny.

Jonas took two quick steps toward me and yanked me toward him. He squeezed me to his chest. "Good work, human. Good job."

"Oh my god, I'm going to be an uncle! Jonas, bro, she's going to have a baby!" Charles screeched. "Put her down. My turn. But be careful!"

Jonas gently lowered me to the ground and stared down at me. The first genuine smile I could remember gracing his lips. His eyes twinkled and all the malice he usually had drifted away. "It's the Boss'?"

I blinked a few times, staring at his smile in confusion. "Y-yeah."

Jonas slid his thumb down my cheek and then kissed my forehead. He passed me off to Charles as if I was the most precious thing he'd ever come across.

I blinked in confusion for the second time. Charles' eyes were glassy. He pulled me into a tight hug, surrounding me in his strength and protection.

"Loosen up, fool, you'll hurt her." Jonas pried Charles' arms away until the hug was lighter. I felt Jonas' hand on my head.

My pants were still around my ankles. Two guys were fawning all over me like grandmothers, in a bathroom, with plastic wands for testing urine in their hands, not worried that my butt was bare. And I was letting all this happen without freaking out.

This had just become the strangest day of my life. And that was saying something.

Jonas said, "Human, pull up your pants. We need to talk about this. This is going to change everything."

CHAPTER FIVE

 $\mathcal{I}$ sat on the couch, opposite of a focused Jonas and a beaming Charles.

I was pregnant.

It wasn't real yet. I hadn't been trying, and hadn't been expecting it, and now I couldn't quite take it all in. I had a hitchhiker in my stomach. It wasn't just me in this body, anymore. Something else was in there with me.

That was the craziest thought.

"I can't take care of a baby!" I blurted out of nowhere before Jonas had even started his lecture. "I can't even take care of myself! I've never even held a baby! I don't know how to change a diaper."

"You don't need to take care of you—that's what we're for," Charles said with soft eyes. "We got this."

"This race covets children," Jonas said in calm tones. "Children are the continuation of our line. Two in seven women in our clan carry to term without miscarriage. One in three of those go on to have more than one, but usually never make it to more than three. That isn't many. Now, with the presence of more humans, that number may rise. But as of right now, there is a thin line connecting our race to the future. And that line is solely tied to women being able to reproduce. We take this very seriously."

My emotions were racing around me, as I worried over what Stefan would say. I was full of fear that I'd ruin someone else's life with the craziness of something growing inside of me right at that very minute...

I needed to drive very fast. Things were so out of control and I needed something that would make me concentrate.

I stood up with that in mind and Jonas and Charles stood up with me. Charles walked to the entrance of the room and crossed his arms over his chest like a guard.

"Human, listen to me," Jonas said with more iron in his voice. "Males have fought each other to the death to be tied to a female and her young. Those males didn't even know whom the child came from, and they didn't care. None of us care. A male will lose his mind to the protective instinct when his mate is pregnant. Given that this is the Boss'—that this is his blood—you will have to put aside your independence for nine months and let him protect you. Let us protect you. Let every member of this clan, male or female, protect you however they can."

"Stefan already protects me," I said in confusion. "You— everyone—already do that."

"Sasha," Charles said from the doorway, "I've seen males cut their female's meat for fear they might not do it right and choke."

Jonas glanced back at Charles with a look promising pain. "Go play with yourself or something. The adults are talking."

"Yeah, real funny, bro. I'm just as much a part of this as you are. I get to help."

Jonas turned back. As soon as his gaze hit mine it softened. The effect unnerved me more than anything else that had happened so far. "A male will cut his female's food, because he wants to start providing. He wants to show the others you are his, and he is taking care of you. The Boss is an alpha—an alpha of alphas—he will exhibit this trait more than others."

"Exhibit, huh? You been reading your dictionary?" Charles muttered.

A flash of irritation stole Jonas' features. He cocked his head before visibly curbing his expression to one of patience for me. "You need to give him more slack, do you get me? He will be irrational at times. You need to pick your battles. A female in this clan would let most things go. She would be expecting this. You are not—this is a great divide between humans and us. You will need to let him..."

"Act like a chick," Charles finished.

Jonas stared at me. Apparently that was the right finish to the sentence. I felt like I was in a twilight zone.

"Fine. Great. Let Stefan go crazy and fuzzy. I can handle that." But I didn't think I could handle much more talk like this.

Charles snickered. "You have no idea, Sasha. You are totally going to flip."

"Shut up, simpleton," Jonas warned. "You're still learning how your dick works. As soon as you grow pubic hair you'll take this seriously."

"Bro, I'm taking this seriously. You just don't know her as well as I do. You weren't there in the beginning. They have an understanding now, sure, but that shit is about to change when he tries to take control again. This is going to be fire-works and kerosene, yo."

"He was there," I corrected him, wiping my brow. "He tried to let the Dulcha kill me, remember?"

"Busted!" Charles yelled. "Such a dick move. Total 180, though. It all worked out. Just sayin'."

Jonas was trying for patience—his smoldering eyes and

clenched fists gave him away. It just wasn't coming as fast this time.

"Oh, and Sasha," Charles continued. "When the Mansion finds out, they'll be crazy, too. Just so you know."

My phone chirped from my handbag near the door. I bounded up and immediately ran into Charles. "What do you need? I'll get it."

"I ain't done, human," Jonas pushed.

"That's probably Ann." I pushed at Charles. "I need girl time. I called her to come over."

"I'll go get her." Charles waited for Jonas to come and play roadblock so he could scoop up my phone and took off out the door.

"Jonas, this is already irritating," I cautioned.

"That's my point. Now, you need to take it easy. Take it slow. And if your body rejects that baby in the first three months, that's okay. You don't need to get down on yourself. It is perfectly natural. Most females lose their first couple of babies."

I slowed down until everything settled. I stared up at Jonas and soaked in his comforting, calming stance. I was barely getting used to the idea of being pregnant myself, and he was telling me I'd probably lose it.

Something clicked over in my head. I hadn't known how to feel, and I wasn't sure about a trespasser inside me, but hearing I might lose him or her shook me. This baby was Stefan's and mine. It was a piece of us. I didn't want to lose it. I needed a moment to stress and panic about being a crappy mother, but I didn't want to lose the life we'd created. I wanted this little peanut, and I would do anything to protect him or her. He or she was a part of our family now.

Jonas put a hand on my shoulder. The comforting warmth seeped into me. In a display of affection that was unusual for him, he reeled me in and held me gently. "The good news is that you are able to get pregnant. That is step one."

"Where is she, Charles?" Ann stormed into the living room a moment later and stopped dead with the sight of Jonas holding me. "What happened?" she whispered in a terrified voice.

"These guys have grown vaginas," I murmured through Jonas' hard chest. "But Jonas is like an electric blanket, and I am surprisingly really comfortable. It helps knowing that he's not trying to get in my pants, of course."

"I only tried until the Boss marked you," Charles said in a huff as he walked in.

"So what's going on?" Ann stood beside us in a fuzzy pink robe. Charles must've snatched it up from my old room.

I struggled out of Jonas' grasp and faced Ann. With a deep breath, I said, "I'm pregnant."

Ann stared at me for a second. "Are you sure?"

"I took two tests."

"Holy shit, Sasha." Ann breathed deeply and put her hands to her hips. "How did this happen?"

Finally! A normal reaction!

"I have no idea," I admitted, taking a couple steps and sinking into the couch. Ann followed in a daze. "I was on the pill."

"I thought these guys weren't even fertile?"

I shrugged. I was just as mystified as she was.

"Ungrateful," Charles growled. "Why are you bringing logic into this? This isn't a place for logic. This is a place for unicorns and cotton candy."

"Charles, you belong in a fun house with your unicorns and cotton candy," Ann retorted. She stared at me. "Scared? Happy?"

"Yes. Both. I don't know anything about this."

"I told you—"

Suddenly Ann was action, cutting Charles off. She jumped off the couch, punched him soundly in the stomach, and pointed a finger toward the door. "Get out! This is a girl conversation. You don't have any part of this. Get out. When all this is hashed out, we'll talk to you."

"What about Jonas?" Charles whined.

"Jonas is being quiet. Besides, he is giving me some terrifying looks. I know your people go fruit-loops over pregnant women—I've seen that weird farm you have—so I know what to expect. But you're just being a mother hen, and that isn't working right now."

"Jesus. Gang up on a guy." With a last look at Jonas, who apparently supported Ann's judgment, Charles left shaking his head. I felt a little bad for him, but in this situation, I just needed a second to digest things. Just one.

"How come you've seen that pregnant farm place?" I asked Ann. "I've never been out there."

"I was helping out the Watch and I don't have the schedule you do."

It was true. With finding humans filling in what should've been the downtime after Andris' takedown, I hadn't even been patrolling. Now I was a little fearful of what I'd be walking into if I spent any time at that weird retreat for pregnant women and families.

"Will we have to move there?" I asked in a whisper.

"First things first," Ann said, sitting down. "How are you feeling? How freaked out? Do you want to get another test just to make sure?"

I settled back and let the world slow around me. I let my emotions align. "It's still weird. I really wasn't planning this."

Ann nodded silently, letting me work around this new discovery.

A feeling of love welled up inside of me with the knowledge that Stefan would be excited. That we had created a piece of us. That we could raise a little troublemaker and have no idea which parent that trait came from. Or if it was both.

A smile formed on my lips as I felt a pulse of love answer my feelings through the blood link. I hadn't realized I'd uncovered the muffle.

"Okay, good. That's good. Phew!" Ann wiped her forehead in a show of relief. "If you didn't want this kid, your life would've been hell, Sasha. Just sayin'."

"Don't speak like that, Ann," Jonas warned.

"Not that it won't still be hell." Ann threw Jonas a look.

"Jonas said that most girls lose the first couple," I said quietly, hoping Ann knew more about this than I did.

"His kind, maybe. You're human, dearie. The first three months are always iffy, which is why a lot of people don't tell anyone. But it's way lower than their people. It's like, twelve per cent or something. So you should probably try to keep it to yourself—"

"Won't happen," Jonas interrupted. "The Boss will want the reproduction specialists checking in with her every day."

"Oh yeah, you're going to hate your life." Ann laughed this time. "They're going to treat you like one of them, when you aren't nearly as fragile as they are. You are going to go bat-shit crazy."

"This isn't a joke, mongrel," Jonas warned.

"Well, if it was, it still wouldn't be funnier than you." Ann grinned at the thunderclouds on his face before turning back to me. "At least these people expect things to go wrong. That takes the pressure off."

"Okay, so...this is going to try my patience."

"Probably. But you'll be treated like royalty—at least the people at that farm were—so I am totally going to hang around you every chance I get."

Everyone fell silent for a moment, pondering what came next.

"Any news on that strange shifter?" I asked.

Jonas leaned forward, his substantial muscles popping as he leaned his elbows on his knees.

"We think he's been around," Ann said in a somber voice. "Your keys turned back up. I immediately brought Tim in to catch the scent. His eyes turned...scary. Very scary. It's definitely an alpha with a lot of power. And he's slinking around Tim's territory. Tim...is...pissed."

"No one saw him?" The shifter compound was like an army barracks. A stranger coming and going wasn't normal.

"Bruce—one of the guys that patrol the compound—saw a blond guy he didn't recognize this morning. He tried to follow the stranger but lost him. Bruce thinks he has some sort of elite forces experience by the way he moved around. Bruce also has elite forces experience, which is how he'd know."

"Boss is going to make sure that filthy animal is taken out," Jonas said with a growl.

"Stefan is letting Tim handle it," Ann argued.

"That was before he knew his mate was carrying his child. He won't allow that sort of danger in his town. Not now."

"Stefan and Tim think this guy might be reporting to someone else," I said.

A shadow passed over Ann's face. "Tim checked in with the other packs. None have had intruders, so it's just us. And this is the only place a shifter community is in close contact with Stefan's kind. It probably isn't a power struggle for alpha, which would mean..."

"Tim and Stefan are probably right. And here I thought it would be quiet without Andris."

Jonas stood in a smooth movement. "Quit stalling, human. Grab one of those tests and let's go see the Boss."

Ann gave me a supportive grin. I exhaled and stood, scrubbing my palm on my jeans as butterflies swirled in my stomach. "Maybe I should plan a nice dinner and tell him then?"

"You need to interrupt whatever he is doing and tell him straight away, human. He will want to know immediately." Jonas put a hand in the air, indicating I was to walk in front of him.

I couldn't help the grin. "What's up, Jonas? Not going to grab me by the collar and shove me along like usual?"

"C'mon, human," Jonas answered.

In other words, no. He was no longer allowed to touch me forcefully. What a lovely course in self-restraint it would be for him. It was going to be a long nine months for a great many people if all the rules were about to change...

I said goodbye to Ann and promised to call her later. Charles was pacing by the door. As soon as he saw us he straightened up and stepped aside, waiting for me to pass in front. "All better now? Done freaking out?"

"We finally have something in common. I'm now as hormonal as you. Only, mine is not from going through puberty."

"Everyone's a comedian," Charles retorted as Jonas' lips tweaked toward a grin.

The cool evening air brushed my face and calmed the raging butterflies. My feet crunched on the dirt and rocks outside the bungalow. I stopped for a moment, relishing the twilight as the shadows stretched across the ground and started to blend together. The night flirted with my magic. Elements danced and played around me, ready to weave into a spell at a moment's notice.

"I love this time," I said in a sigh. "When the day is shaking hands with the night. I feel it's like the middle between my two halves—my past life and my future."

"Your past life was just a classroom. This is where you belong. Where you've always belonged. You just had to slog through shit to be worthy of it." Jonas looked out at the trees, lines of fatigue and exhaustion ringing his eyes.

"How'd you guys know where to find me?" I asked as a few crickets started their chorus. I could hear voices in the direction of the Mansion.

"Got the call you'd left. Charles phoned the mongrels and told them to look out for you. After that, we got word of a couple of sightings," Jonas answered.

"That Tim has got a tight network, I'll say that," Charles murmured. He'd inched closer to me since I stopped walking. His gaze was on my stomach. "Since last night he has people everywhere. Still hasn't caught that intruder, though. The guy must be good."

"The mongrel is new. Boss has been around a while. If there's someone that don't belong here, the Boss will chase him out." Jonas' jaw clenched. "No one messes with one of our pregnant females."

"Wow." I couldn't help the widened eyes. I was about to say more when I saw a hand slowly, gently, land on my stomach. I swiveled my head with an inquiring raised eyebrow at Charles.

"Sasha, don't freak out. This is totally normal."

"Charles, creeping closer to lay your hand on my belly doesn't exactly sound totally normal. Especially since my stomach is flat."

After a beat I added an, "Ish," just to be mostly correct. "Flat-ish."

He took his hand away just as slowly. "Note taken."

"We good, or what? We gonna stand here all night?" Jonas asked. That irritation was peeking through again. He was having a really hard time with this patience issue.

The butterflies started up again as I pushed forward. The

trees rustled from a small stirring of wind. As we passed the stone benches where I liked to sit to take in the dawn on occasion, Jonas said, "That human male has a mix of our blood and human. He said it was from his father."

"What about his power level?" I asked in a hush, slowing again as we approached the door where a few people stood chatting.

"She thinks as high as gold. Probably light gold." Jonas' jaw clenched as he matched my slower pace.

"We did good, Sasha." Charles veered in close again. "It's way easier to train halvsies."

"Are there many?" I asked, thinking of Delilah.

"Not that we can find. You heard Paulie's story," Charles reminded me, his hand reaching toward me slowly. I slapped it away. "They don't mention what they see in the shadows once they've been called crazy. And because of the pheromones, the human females don't realize where the baby came from. Which I had never realized was a little fucked up before."

I slapped his hand away again.

"I am going to make you some bright orange booties," Charles promised.

I took it as a threat.

"We lose access to children that way," Jonas said in a tight voice. He cleared his throat with burning eyes. His fists tightened.

I couldn't help a grin. He totally wanted to push me through the door and throw Charles in after me. His face was nearly puce with the effort of holding back.

"Does he count as human, though? Does his magic count as human's?" I asked. If he veered towards Stefan's race, it wouldn't work in a large link.

"Could go either way." A line formed between Jonas' eyebrows in thought. "I have to ask Selene about the taste.

Humans taste a little more savory and our kind a bit sweeter."

"Savory, huh? Charles! Stop touching me! It's getting weird. I don't even have a bump."

"Can't help it. It's exciting." Charles put his hands in his pockets with an excited smile. "No one ever lets me around pregnant females."

"You are like a damn dog, Charles. Did you ever realize that?"

"Get used to it, human. He won't be the only one trying to touch you." Jonas shifted in impatience. "Now, are you ready? Standing around out here is getting nothing done. We need to check in with the Boss, and arrange for you to see the doctor. Then we can decide what things you can still do."

"What things I can still do?" I asked quietly, turning toward Jonas.

"That's the look, right there, bro!" Charles pointed at my face and started laughing. "Get used to that one. You're going to see that a lot." Through chuckles, Charles continued with, "C'mon, Sasha, the father needs to know."

Charles was right. Stefan didn't deserve to be the last to know, and if Charles kept trying to shake hands with my unborn child, the whole house would know before Stefan did.

With another swarm of butterflies hatching, I headed into the house.

CHAPTER SIX

Stefan sat at the head of the table in the hushed room. Jameson had gone through their territory and identified the efforts of the Mata. The beasts had been sighted all over the grid, often tracking and crossing back, on a trail that wasn't a straight line. While Tim's efforts and his call to arms was commendable, he was still learning his post. His people weren't practiced. If this guy was half as good as he seemed, he'd be able to evade them.

"Have we identified the intruder?" Stefan asked, leaning back in his chair. A wave of nervous energy bled through the blood link from Sasha. Whatever she was doing, she wasn't comfortable with it.

Probably a new spell that would piss Jonas off in some way.

"We have his scent and his shape. A black panther—Sasha was right about the big cat." Jameson put a mark on the map to identify the sightings. "We've also run into scents from our own kind."

Stefan sat forward. "What do you mean?"

Jameson marked the large map with red dots, all fairly

well spaced apart. "I think our kind is checking us out, and using this Mata intruder somehow. We have no proof of this —and this is just me speculating—but the two scents meet up occasionally." Jameson pointed out where a red and black dot met.

"Teamed with Cato's growing concern and Dominicous questioning our defenses..." Stefan let the thought trail away. "Something's coming."

Jameson's lips formed a white line. Everyone else around the table shifted. Take out one enemy, you gain two more. Is a quiet life so much to ask for?

"We need to know who's in my territory," Stefan stated, feeling Sasha drawing closer. "I want to leave Tim to work on his shifter problem, though. He needs the experience."

"I'm thinking Sasha can be of some use at the sites of their meet-ups. See if they were working with anything magical."

Stefan was about to agree with Jameson when the door to the strategy room opened. Sasha peeked in with large eyes. He stood and walked to her immediately, angling his body so she knew she was welcomed.

"Uh, Stefan, can I talk to you, please?" she asked quietly, traces of fear and uncertainty bleeding through the link.

"Privately?" he asked, using the same volume.

"Yes, please." She smiled at Jameson, and then around the table at a few members of the Watch. "Sorry, you guys. This'll just take a moment."

"Of course, Mage," Jameson said, bowing his head.

Another shot of anxiety pulsed through the link. Stefan followed her out into the hall, catching sight of Jonas and Charles at a distance. Which was unusual. Generally, if she was with him, they made themselves scarce without his having to dismiss them.

"Um. We'll just…go to that bench, okay?" Sasha wrung her hands, not meeting his gaze.

"Are you okay?" Stefan wrapped his arm around her shoulders.

"Go to the bungalow, human," Jonas instructed as if he were in charge of her decisions.

A blast of irritation welled up in Stefan. Before he could rectify the situation, though, Charles said, "Easy does it, Boss. This'll all make sense soon. Nice and gentle."

Another blast of nervousness came through the link from Sasha.

Tendrils of fear began to work its way through to him. Jonas and Charles were acting as if they needed to be there to protect her. From him? She was not comfortable with whatever she had to say and the males didn't think he'd be rational about it. It couldn't be good news.

Willing calm, he let his mate lead him out into the fading light of evening and to the concealed house. There, she sat him in the exact spot she'd accepted his offer to be his mate, and sat beside him. Silence descended around them. She wouldn't meet his eyes.

"So, um." Sasha cleared her throat and glanced up. Their gazes met and his heart started to thump, the reaction he always had to her.

A small, embarrassed smile lit up her face as red colored her cheeks. "Uh," she tried again.

He leaned forward and brushed her lips with his. He couldn't help it. Then, equally not able to help it, he deepened the kiss, forgetting entirely about his misgivings. His hands roamed up under her sweatshirt and over her perky breasts. She moaned into his mouth and leaned back. He let his hand slip low to her thigh and then up, rubbing her apex through her jeans.

He unbuttoned her jeans, shifted so he could slide her

pants lower, and slipped his fingers along her slit. She was so warm and wet. So delicious.

Taking her jeans off the rest of the way, he leaned her back and settled between her legs, licking up through her hot core. He sucked at the top, making her mew like a kitten. He worked in two fingers and sucked, loving the rise and fall of her hips. And her panting. He worked her harder until she ran her fingers through his hair and gripped.

"Oh, Stefan," she moaned, going rigid as she rode an orgasm.

Stefan pulled her up quickly and stripped off her sweatshirt and shirt. He discarded her bra and sucked deeply on one of her nipples. Her fingers were at his pants, tugging. Pulling them down. She stripped off his shirt. A trail of warmth followed her hands as they covered his body. She rose up so he could grab the base of his shaft and line up. Nibbling his lips, she sat down slowly.

Her body was so hot and tight. So welcoming and wet. He couldn't contain his need. One hand cupping her breast, he put the other on her butt and lifted. He slid out of her before pushing her back down. His erection thrusting back in.

"Mmm," she moaned.

Her hips began to rock, and then moved in circles. She created more friction as she bounced, squeezing his manhood as she sat down on him. She felt so good. Being deep inside her body was heaven.

With hands on her hips, he lifted her and sat her back down. Then again. Over and over. Their bodies slapped together. Her mews of delight grew louder. His tip started to tingle. His balls tightened up. He needed to finish.

He lifted her again, and then thrust as he was pulling her down.

"Oh holy—" Her head fell back.

He lifted, brought her down, and thrust again.

"Oh, my God. Oh, holy—OH!"

Stefan's whole body blasted apart with the last thrust. Her core squeezed him tightly, milking him dry. He emptied into her completely, happily sated.

"Oh my God," Sasha whispered as she laid on his chest.

"I love you," he said softly, burying his face into her neck. "But I ruined your news. What did you want to tell me?"

"I love you. And we've had an accident. I'm pregnant."

He felt a sweet kiss as the news sank in. Then his heart stopped.

"You're what?" He froze. His heart started again, but now it was pounding erratically. Sweat erupted on his brow as his stomach started to turn. "Did you say you're pregnant?"

Sasha pushed herself back slowly, fear creeping into her expression. Tears glistened in her eyes. "Are you mad? I didn't mean for this to happen, Stefan! I swear. I was on the pill." A tear leaked out, twisting his gut.

"No, no, no. Shh—shhh. It's okay. This is my fault. I interrupted you. I shouldn't have interrupted you." Without moving her body, trying to keep her in exactly the same position, he got up with her wrapped around his waist and thrashed out of his pants.

"What are you doing?" she asked, clutching onto his shoulders. "Are you mad?"

"It's okay. This is probably okay. You're human, so hopefully I didn't totally fuck up. I should've waited. Just stay calm, baby. This is fine." Still in her body, afraid to come out lest he witness first-hand what he'd just done, he walked to the door with his heart in his throat. Trying not to jar her, he opened the front door gingerly and, as calmly as possible so as not to frighten her, he stepped out onto the porch.

"Stefan?" she asked with uncertainty. She turned around to see where they were going.

"It's okay." He was reassuring himself more than her.

Jonas turned at the sound of the door opening. He took one glance at them and yelled, "Charles, go get the doctor!"

"What happened?" Charles ducked around the corner. "What the fuck, Boss? What the fuck—"

"Get the doctor!" Jonas yelled with a ferocity usually reserved for battle.

"What's happening?" Sasha whimpered, tears running down her face. Fear bled through the link.

"No, no. It's okay!" Stefan said in a soothing voice. "It'll be fine. Is she bleeding Jonas?"

Stefan couldn't look. He couldn't look down. If he'd just destroyed his unborn child he would never forgive himself.

"Bleeding?" Sasha asked in confusion.

Jonas ducked down next to them.

"What is he doing?" Sasha screeched, dropping her hand to try and push Jonas away.

"It's okay, baby. He's just checking to see. Are you cramping? How does everything feel? Is there pain anywhere?"

"She's okay," Jonas proclaimed. "We'll get the doctor in and have a look just to be sure."

Stefan closed his eyes with a huge sigh.

"Stefan, what the hell has gotten into you? It was just sex. That's not going to shake anything loose." Sasha threw up a magical barrier between them and Jonas, making it a deep black. It was a censor bar. "Take me back inside, please. This is ridiculous. How gross is this? I can't have Jonas checking out my junk! Especially like this! God, this day goes from weird to weirder."

"Boss, do you want me inside?" Jonas asked.

Suddenly, his behavior earlier made perfect sense. Here was a male that knew his job, and would do it regardless of Stefan's reaction.

A warm feeling of confidence infused Stefan's stomach as he turned into the house. He thought his baby had a protector for life outside his or her immediate family. Stefan wished he'd been so lucky when he had been a kid. Sasha probably did, too.

Back in the house, Stefan settled them gently onto the couch. He was still afraid to take himself out until the doctor got there, which was all cowardice in case something had happened and no logic, so he sat with her still clinging to him and gently restrained her from moving off.

"Stefan, I can still have sex when pregnant. I don't know much, but I do know that much." Her eyebrows were low over her eyes, berating, but elation tickled their link. Her eyes sparkled and her cheeks turned red. "You're happy, though?"

Stefan couldn't speak. He didn't want to cry like a little girl. Instead, he laid his palm on the side of her face. Then, shaking, he moved his hand slowly downward between them until he was gently resting it on her flat stomach. He felt like the luckiest male in the world. It was not only his baby because she was his mate, but it was actually his baby. From his body. His blood. Their mingled blood.

He couldn't help the lump in his throat. Nor the stinging in his eyes.

Sasha's smile was the most beautiful thing he'd ever seen. "I love you so much," he said, choking up and falling silent. It was the safest way to maintain his manhood.

What he would tell her, when he could, was that this baby would want for nothing. Not ever. If he died tomorrow, this baby would always be taken care of. As would she. Forever. Not one person on this earth would ever touch a hair on their heads. Not one. He had loved no one like he loved Sasha, and now he couldn't imagine even what the word love meant. It was too small a word to encompass his feelings. Not the swelling that started in his heart and ran the length of him, so deep, so pure.

"I love you," he tried again, his voice shaking.

Nope, not ready yet.

He could wrangle his past and come out on top. He could stare a demon in the face and growl. He could take on an army of overwhelming odds with nothing more than a grimace. But he couldn't hear that his mate was having his baby and not sob like a child.

No one had told him it would feel like this. No one could've possibly prepared him for this moment.

With a deep breath, he clutched her to his chest and just held on. His wildest dreams were coming true, and he'd rip apart the world to make sure these two people were safe.

CHAPTER SEVEN

I blinked into the murkiness of our bedroom. Judging by the light, it was a couple hours before nightfall. I registered the warm palm on my stomach, sending the vibes of safety through my core. Stefan's heat lined my right side. His even breathing was the only sound in the room.

I closed my eyes again, so contented with his presence I didn't want to leave it.

It had been four months of quiet since we found out I was pregnant. No one had heard or smelled the strange lurking shifter around. It was as if he had done some homework on Charles and me, and then taken off. While that brought up a lot of questions and speculation, it was actually an extremely good thing, because like Jonas and Charles had said, everything changed once Stefan and the Mansion found out I was pregnant.

I was no longer allowed to do much. And while that would usually piss me off, for a wonder, this hadn't. In fact, I wasn't having the reactions Charles and Ann thought I would to all the change. Well, not as far as Stefan was concerned, anyway. When he had me sit in on one of his boring meetings because he didn't want me out of his sight, I would normally have rolled my eyes and tried to blast him across the room. For the last four months, though? Meek as a lamb.

I went willingly, almost gladly, when he insisted we compromise on duties so we could be in each other's presence constantly. I allowed him to carry me up stairs. I didn't baulk when he held my plate to collect dinner in the common eating room. And yes, I even allowed the guy to cut my meat.

My mate cut my meat like I was a child, and for some reason, I was not only okay with this, I was comforted by it.

Comforted by it!

I cringed from myself every time I thought of it. But when I was in the moment, it all seemed so natural.

Toa had given me one of his long lectures on the phone, explaining that my sudden desire to be treated as a princess was to do with our blood link, and with my understanding of his primal need to take care of me and protect me. And that was probably true. This certainly seemed like animalistic behavior. But I still couldn't think about it with a level head without blinking in confusion. I hardly even knew myself.

This was only the case with Stefan, though. With anyone else, I was still a cranky ol' sod who didn't want to be told what to do. I was surprised Jonas hadn't had a heart attack!

I soaked in the waves of love and safety promised by Stefan's presence. I felt my body hum with his touch. I felt the soft flutters of our baby as it swirled within my growing belly. And I felt a peace I'd never known settle on me like a soft, warm blanket. My sigh expressed my absolute bliss of this moment and of the million moments I'd had in these past four months.

Unfortunately, I also felt like I was going to wet the bed.

I eased myself out of the covers so as not to wake Stefan. I knew I only had a short time before I could get back in bed without him waking up—any distance had him looking around, wondering where I'd gone. I hurried to the bath-room, did my deal, and came back to find his eyes open and his gaze monitoring my progress.

"Good morning, beautiful. How do you feel?" he asked, rising.

"Oh." I stopped halfway to the bed. "Are you getting up?"

He froze. "No? Are you coming back to bed?"

I smiled like an idiot and continued my journey to his side. He stood and opened his arms for me to fill. "I thought maybe we could take a walk before we started our day," Stefan said, laying his cheek on the top of my head.

I rested my cheek against his chest and listened to the steady beat of his heart. I let my eyes drift closed as his strength surrounded me and held me close. "Sounds good," I murmured.

"Cato is getting antsy, so I also thought we should work with the humans, today. Get some more people in that link, and then try and merge with me."

"Sounds good," I murmured again.

His chuckle was deep and pleasant. "Okay, let's brave the halls."

I leaned back and tilted up my chin, losing myself in Stefan's deep and dark eyes. He leaned down slowly and brushed his lips against mine. Then he deepened the kiss, opening my mouth with his and slipping in his tongue. Before I knew it, I was moaning and holding onto him, feeling his hard length push against me. I lifted my leg and hooked my thigh around his waist. Needing him. Needing his body inside of mine.

After a brief hesitation with the constant fear that sex might hurt the baby, Stefan let his lust and logic overcome the problems of his people. I felt his tip rub against my swollen sex, parting my folds with his velvety warmth. He eased into me slowly, the glorious girth of him lighting fires inside me.

Some women had no desire for sex during pregnancy. Some couldn't get enough. I was one of the latter. Or maybe I couldn't get enough of Stefan, I had no idea. But making love now was better than it had ever been.

I clutched onto his shoulders and lifted my other leg. He grabbed it immediately and curved it around his waist, holding me up. Gently but firmly, he thrust into me. The deep slide of his manhood made my head fall back and my nipples tingle. His lips left a hot trail down my neck. He sucked in at the base of my throat, right over my vein.

I rocked my hips upwards and back, creating more friction. "Mmm, Stefan," I sighed, my eyes fluttering. My body heated up as he moved inside me. My moans became louder. "Faster," I breathed.

Still as gently as he was able, he quickened his pace until his body was softly hitting against mine. Our breath mingled as our lips touched. His tongue licked my lower lip. His body filled me up, over and over, thrusting. Sending shooting sparks. Sending me to the edge.

"Oh God, Stefan," I begged, working my body. Working his manhood. I tore at his neck and took a long pull of the sweetest taste I'd ever experienced. Stefan groaned. His arms tightened around me. He thrust into me harder. So deep. It felt so good.

"YES!" Blasts of pleasure filled my body as the orgasm overcame me. I took another long suck until he grunted in ecstasy and shivered in completion.

The clan doctor said he shouldn't take my blood during pregnancy, but that taking his was natural and healthy for the growing fetus. For some reason, the taste had turned into something better than a dessert. I craved it, sometimes walking to him in the middle of a meeting, as if I was dreaming, sitting in his lap, and sucking his blood. Crazier? Everyone paused so I could satisfy myself. He welcomed me, took pleasure in my need of him, and everyone else waited patiently until I was done.

The place was a loony bin. Ann wanted to hear stories daily because she flat-out didn't believe it. But yet...it was my life.

"The entire clan is jealous of me, did Jonas tell you?" Stefan asked as he got dressed a moment later. He slipped a black tee shirt over his gloriously sculpted chest.

"Always have been. When you're mated to awesome-sauce, what did you expect?" I slipped into some designer sweats. I was starting to show now and none of my pants fit. Rather than maternity clothes, for now I was wearing sweats. The designer label meant I could get away with it without Ann making fun of me and calling me a soccer mom.

"Not only are you having my baby but I am still allowed to make love to you. Usually females are off limits."

"I had no idea you guys had such a hard time procreating. I mean, I knew it because you'd said so, but I didn't know you guys were so fragile. I wonder why that is."

Stefan shrugged and waited for me to be ready. When I was, he threaded his fingers through mine and led me out of the room. "They marvel at how robust you are."

"Robust? What the hell! I'm all baby right now. I only have a potbelly! They're the bricks of muscle."

Stefan laughed as we took the elevator down—he didn't like me exerting myself on the stairs. And yes, this seemed normal too.

Get away, logic!

"Robust meaning tough. Aside from the morning sickness, which is normal, you've had no problems. You are healthy, no bleeding, and you run and use magic. A quarter of our females end up laying down for half their pregnancy."

"Maybe you guys should move out of your clan a little more. Get some fresh bloodlines through here. I mean, we don't need to create an Arkansas situation through here..."

I waited for the laughter with an open mouth and raised eyebrows. What I got was a confused look and, "Was that a human joke?"

"Well, Delilah's got her own breeding project underway." He just didn't realize how funny I was. That was the problem.

"She's a month along, I hear."

Delilah had been successful with her man, who had only waited to mate her after she was pregnant because he was worried he couldn't knock her up. After hearing about Stefan's reaction, she wanted to try for the same thing. There were now two guys who knew, without a doubt, that their mate was having their baby. And while Tom was usually more of a beta, submitting readily to the more dominant males, he'd experienced quite a makeover where his mate was concerned. He threw some guy across the room that tried to entice Delilah over to his hearth, stating he could take better care of her. She didn't even bat an eye at the violence.

We were cracked.

Seriously, get away logic!

"The clan is looking at humans in a different light, now," Stefan said with pride.

"Selene is trying to get Paulie to mate her."

"He's..." Stefan paused as someone veered in toward me with a smile.

It was a youngish male still in school, probably up early for chores or to get a few more hours in before a test. With sparkling eyes he said, "Hia Mage. May I?"

He didn't wait for a response. No one ever did.

The young guy put his palm on my bump and gave a little rub. "Good luck, young one. Hope to meet you soon!"

And then he was off, walking down the hall as if he'd just rubbed Buddha's belly.

"I'm okay with you being overbearing, but I could really do without all the communal touching," I grumbled as we made our way outside.

Stefan chuckled softly. "Paulie will be an excellent fighter." Stefan led me out to the trees as the failing light sprinkled across the ground. Wind rustled the trees high overhead. The sky blazed pinks and oranges.

"Thank God his magic comes from his mother or I'd be down a strong human."

"I don't know for sure that it comes from his mother. But it's introverted, definitely. We're still repairing the wall for Master Bert. He wasn't thrilled about his classroom being destroyed."

Paulie had wasted no time getting the special runes that could throw magic. The guy was already covered in tattoos so what were a few dozen more? He'd also wasted no time learning to work the elements. With me helping, and Charles and Jonas tweaking the way he went about things, the guy was already the best human at working with magic besides me. Selene had misjudged him a little—it turned out he was orange but my special trait had him pushing up into a light gold. Even still, he was seriously a huge find.

And he was sexing his way through the Mansion. Oh, he still liked Selene best, it seemed, but he had taken a page out of Charles' book. The guy was like a kid in the candy store, and with Delilah and I having been knocked up so quickly in their opinion, all the ladies were lining up. It was actually comical.

"I think the linking is going pretty well," I said as I stood in a patch of sunlight and let the last rays of the day shine down on me. I felt a flutter inside me. "I think the baby likes the light, too."

Stefan's eyes went gooey as his gaze dipped to my stomach. He rested his palm on my bump. "When will I get to feel him or her?"

"I don't know. You'll have to ask the midwife. You know, that woman who unnecessarily checks in with me daily? The one who comes right after the doctor who also unnecessarily checks in with me daily?" I would've tapped my foot but I was too busy soaking up the warmth of the moment, both from Stefan's touch and the sun.

"Here comes Jonas," Stefan said to deflect my light rebuff.

"Boss, Human—this doesn't count as walking. She needs to exercise." He stopped beside us with a disapproving scowl.

"Jesus, Mabel, let's calm down with the overbearing behavior, huh?" I felt Stefan's tug and dutifully began to walk. But not because of Jonas. I made sure he understood that fact with a glare.

Delilah did what everyone told her. My meekness was limited to Stefan.

"Humans will be here at nine thirty," Jonas informed us. "One of the twins can't make it—she couldn't find a sitter for Aurora."

"I'm sure someone here would be happy to watch her," I reflected, taking the path through the trees deeper into the wooded property. Aurora was Jen's three-year-old and universally loved in the Mansion.

"She needs to go to bed. But we have everyone else coming in, so we should be...fine." I could hear the clenched jaw.

"Jonas, I'm telling you—the link isn't hard for me to hold. I've already worked with that much magic. I just draw off the energy."

"It's still no occupation for a pregnant female."

"Oh yeah? And when did you graduate from medical school?"

"He's just looking after you," Stefan hedged softly.

"Well, I need to work on that link. Paulie is still a little volatile—he needs to work with others more than me."

"The human male bested three members on the Third Tier Watch," Jonas said over my head to Stefan. He then laid his hand on my stomach and gave a little rub.

My stomach was no longer my own property.

"I heard. He's a natural. Any idea who might've sired him?" Stefan asked, now letting me lead to my favorite copse of trees.

"None. With the blood mixed with human, there's really no way to tell."

"Have you let everyone know that pheromones are no longer to be used in sexual...situations?" I turned to Jonas and gave him the full weight of my stare.

Jonas stared back, that glimmer of craziness turning in his depths. "Yes, human. The problem is, humans don't see us. Seduction is then impossible."

"Only if you got no game." I winked at him, earning a deep scowl.

"I got game." Charles walked up with an easy glide. His knitting supplies were in a bag around his shoulder. He no longer cared about carrying something resembling a purse. Why? Well, because he had important business making hideous blankets, scarves and hats for the baby.

He seemed to think babies wore scarves...

"You got problems," Jonas shot back. "Took you long enough to find us. What'd you do, track with your fingers?"

"Nah. I saw you headed this way so thought I might grab some breakfast first. I knew the Boss was with her."

Jonas face turned red as he stared at Charles.

"No fighting in front of pregnant females, bro." Charles grinned.

A vein pulsed in Jonas' jaw.

Smiling, Charles stepped forward and rubbed my belly. "Anyway, what's up for today?"

I let Stefan answer as I cherished the last minutes of the day. My magic rolled along the ground to expand my reach, feeling nature throb within the elements. I flicked and twisted off a couple spells creating colorful bubbles of light just for a way to interact. As the shadows swallowed up the ground, I did one hard pulse to reach that little farther before getting ready to pull it all back in. Spreading my magical awareness out so far was draining, but Toa said I should constantly push to improve my overall reach.

As I opened my eyes to lead the way back to the Mansion, I felt it. That magic. The shifter magic I'd felt four months ago.

Tim had been searching, and since Stefan found out he was going to be a dad, he'd been looking, too. No one had turned up any results. It was as if the guy knew he was being sought by the entire magical community, which was why he took off.

This guy was every bit as smart and trained as Tim and Stefan feared. Not to mention cunning and harboring some sort of agenda that had been devised out of town. He obviously had business here, because I knew for a fact that it was him. He was back. On our property.

"It's that shifter," I said in a hush.

Jonas and Stefan fell silent. Charles froze mid-rub.

"He's here. Way on the outskirts of our property." I focused my magic in that area, feeling his wisps of magic.

"The shifter who followed you?" Stefan growled. Jonas already had his phone to his ear.

"Yeah. He's sitting in one spot." I worked the elements for a cage to trap him, but with the distance I couldn't be sure where exactly he was. It was like a blind man feeling the edges of a telephone. The guy would feel me poking and prodding him with magic. I said as much.

"Then don't. Keep track of him." Stefan put a possessive hand on my shoulder as Jameson came sprinting through the trees already dressed in battle garb. These men could get ready like firemen.

"Did you alert the Watch?" Stefan asked Jameson.

Jameson only had eyes for me. "Yes. They are getting ready and will be getting in position on all sides of that varmint. What do we do with her? Take her to the Farm?"

"These are shifters—strange shifters. They won't give a crap about the truce with our own kind and pregnant females." Charles still had a hold of my belly. "Tim even asked why they weren't protected. He doesn't get it even though he respects it. If we take Sasha there, we'll need to take an arsenal."

I felt movement. A slow, purposeful movement toward the Mansion. Night had fallen, now concealing a black cat like nothing else would. "He's coming this way."

"If we surround him, he's still a cat. On four legs. He's bound to be fast and agile." I got the familiar tingle of battle coming, and a wave of unfamiliar vulnerability. I could run and leap and fight, not caring what happened to me, but now I had someone else to think about. Someone hitching a ride.

"This is terrible timing," I muttered.

"Call Tim," Stefan barked.

"On it," Jonas responded.

"Get her into the Mansion," Stefan said with a savagery I'd rarely heard. "Get some vicious members of the Watch around her. Get Paulie, too. She'll need his power for a link, and he's expressed that he owes her for giving him a sort of family. A loyalty bond is strong with street humans—use it."

"Should I stay with her, Boss?" Charles asked, one hand on my back, one still on my belly.

"Yes. Jonas, with me. I can feel him now. He must be coming closer. I want to trap him. Tim can have his day, but if he fails, I'm taking over."

A shiver went up my back as Charles gently pushed me back toward the Mansion. "C'mon, mama. We have to find Paulie then get you settled. That freaking male is trying to show me up in the prowess department. Did I tell you that? He's got a ways to go, though. He might have magical sperm, but I can still make the girls scream louder."

"Oh, good. I'm going to be hidden away from a stalker with you. What a wonderful start to my night."

"I can hear the sarcasm, Sasha."

"Well, good, because I was laying it on pretty thick."

I had an unnatural fear that something would happen to Stefan. That this panther wasn't what he seemed, and my mate would be in danger.

CHAPTER EIGHT

*P*aulie slid his palm up Selene's perfect form. He felt her perky breast and tweaked a nipple. Her moan made him reach behind her neck and pull her forward, smashing their lips together. With one hand, he guided her toned body over him so he could position his tip at her opening. He guided her body down onto his shaft, plunging deep into her wetness.

"Hmm, yes," she sighed with eyes closed.

She moved her hips in a figure eight, working his dick in a way he'd never experienced before. Not even with other women in this Mansion. He moved within her, a glorious friction along his sensitive shaft tightening his stomach. He thrust upward, banging into her as she sat down on him, hard and fast.

"That's right," she said, a small smile curving her perfect lips. "Hmm, just like that."

His balls started to tingle with anticipation when his phone rang. "Come on," he muttered, not able to stop.

He thrust into her harder. Her tight insides stroked him. Her mews grew louder and more aggressive.

The phone fell silent then started ringing again.

A swear riding a groan, Paulie stood in a rush and then threw Selene down onto the bed. She giggled in delight and reached for him. "Hang on, baby," he said as he snatched his phone off the dresser. The face lit up with Charles' name.

"Yeah?" he asked in annoyance.

"Wipe that tone out of your voice," Charles commanded. Power and authority rode his words, something he rarely heard when Charles was with Sasha since Sasha outranked him. It meant he was speaking from his position as Watch Captain, and not as bodyguard.

Shit.

"Sorry, sir. What do you need?"

"That shifter's back. The Boss wants Sasha quarantined. Meet me in the red library."

"The shifter from that park?" Paulie clarified. He couldn't help an uneasy feeling ice over his intestines.

"That's what Sasha said. He's lingering around in the trees, coming closer. We have no idea why."

"Yes, sir. When?"

"Now."

Air replaced words. He'd hung up. As Paulie turned back to the beauty laying spread eagle on her bed, her phone rang. A beautiful smile turned into a confused frown as her focus completely shifted to the phone on her nightstand. She hadn't even hesitated like he had.

That was an ego crusher.

"Yes, sir?" she answered.

Paulie jumped into his clothes as he tried to spread his magic out like he had been shown. It wasn't easy. He was pretty good with the elements, but getting his magic to spread out from his body to gain information was like sucking ice cream through a straw. Sasha was so much more advanced than anyone in the Mansion, including the teachers, and she didn't even know it.

"We got a shifter loose," Selene said, jumping up with a vicious light in her eyes.

His dwindling hard-on sprang back to life.

"I have to go to the Mage," he said, stepping toward her with a goodbye kiss.

She ignored him as she strapped on some leathers. "Guard her with your life. She is carrying important cargo. She should be at the farm with the others, but we can guard her better here, so I get where the Boss is coming from."

"Okay, well—"

Selene strapped on a sword, winked at him, and said, "Happy hunting."

He stared after her for a moment. It figured. The first time he starts to care about a girl, and she's less sensitive than he is. Irony.

Paulie strapped on his own sword and hit the hallway at a jog. Fierce eyed warriors were rushing around, taking up defensive positions or getting out of the way if they weren't needed. The Boss was a scary sonuvabitch, but he knew how to organize this place. It meant he was smart, confident, and great at his job. If Paulie had been that shifter, he would be steering clear of this territory by now. The fight wouldn't be worth the end result.

He found the library and noticed the paintings had a blue theme. Wrong library.

The place was a maze. These people didn't need half these rooms, let alone ten libraries. Why did they all need books? Would a pool table or air hockey table go amiss?

Hurrying, he backtracked and ducked into another library. It didn't hold Charles and Sasha. He then realized that he had no idea which library the red one was.

He jogged through the front of the Mansion on his way to

the next library when a crawling sensation overcame him. Like red ants running up his spine, biting down as they did so, he knew danger was near.

Paulie slowed and faced the front of the house.

"There you are! What the fuck took you so long? Come through here," Charles said as he poked his head out of a doorway.

"We got trouble." Paulie swept the room for windows but it had none. He took two quick steps to the door and peered back out.

Charles' eyes lost focus as he took a step back. "Something's out there. Go check it out and report back as soon as you can. Don't engage."

"Yes, sir."

"Call when you're back in the library if we're not there," Charles barked.

Paulie was running only a moment later. He thundered through two sitting rooms and into the front area. Only one guy was hanging out at the newly installed desk, staring through the window with round eyes.

"What do you see?" Paulie asked the guy.

"I swear to the gods that big yellow eyes just peered in through that window."

Paulie couldn't help a half-cocked smile. "And you didn't get up to go look?"

"Look, man. I'm used to swords and spells. I'm not used to disembodied yellow eyes staring at me through the window. What was I going to tell Jameson? That I saw a ghost?"

"That you saw a shifter, you fool. Who's the human here, you or me? You should know this shit by now. They've also got one out back." Paulie put his face in the window and noticed an animal jogging out of sight. He felt eyes, though.

He swept his gaze along the street and slowed in the spot

that made his spine tingle. But nothing stared back. Something waited, watching the house. He could swear it. His sixth sense had never let him down on the street. But all he saw was gracefully swaying trees, dancing in the wind.

"You see anything else?" Paulie asked the guard.

"Just those eyes."

Paulie threw the lock on the door and jogged back the way he came. "Let the Boss know we got an animal in the front. If they try to come in, sound some kind of alarm."

"Yes, sir."

Paulie had absolutely no authority, but he didn't plan to mention that. It was just easier that way.

He found his way into the right room and glanced around. A huge rack of books dominated the back wall. A couch and a few chairs were positioned near the middle of the room with a large, mahogany desk sitting against the other wall. But there were no people.

"Where the hell—" He brought up his phone as he noticed the angle of the painting behind the desk. A black crack ran along a white wall. A hidden door. Very smooth.

Paulie ripped it open and shut it behind him. He was plunged in blackness immediately, having him stumbling with the sudden change. As his eyes adjusted, he could just make out a faint glow ahead of him.

Jogging once again, and bouncing off a wall he followed the glow until the passageway dumped him out into a spacious room with two couches facing each other. Sasha sat on one, staring off toward the front of the house, and Charles sat next to her with one hand resting on her belly. Large and silent bodies lingered around the walls, silent and watching. Here for Sasha's protection, obviously.

"Chicks don't like it when you're always touching their belly," Paulie observed as he sauntered into the room.

This was Sasha's jurisdiction, now, and she didn't function

well when everyone was too serious. It made her get lost in her head, and then she made mistakes. This had been drilled into him by Charles and Jonas since that first night Sasha had brought him home.

"Not her belly. It's the clan's belly." Charles looked up with that commanding air. "What'd you see?"

"Shifter in the front. It was on the move. And something else—I don't know for sure what it was, but usually I have a sixth sense where it concerns danger. It felt like something waited outside, but I didn't see anything."

"Shit," Sasha spat. "Probably an invisibility spell. Not good. That means it is Stefan's kind, and they have someone with a high power level and knowledge. I should be out there. No one else knows how to unravel that spell."

"No way is this a threat to the Boss, Sasha," Charles said in a soothing voice. He rubbed her belly. To Paulie, he said, "She's worried for her mate. It's normal for pregnant females to obsess about the safety of their—"

"I'm not obsessing! I'm ready to blow shit up!" Sasha flung Charles' hand off her stomach.

"Now, that's not very nice."

"I don't want them sneaking in here," Sasha said, her focus now on the front of the house. "They're getting close. I have a feeling they want—someone just changed. Did you feel that, guys? That huge blast of power? Changed into human, I'd bet. Probably to open a door and have a gawk. Being naked won't even make this person stand out."

She jumped up. "C'mon, we gotta stop that guy from coming in here. I don't know what they're looking for, but I'm not letting them find it."

"No, no, no, Sasha!" Charles hopped up beside her and put out a restraining hand. Those lingering by the walls all took quick steps in front of hallways and openings, blocking her in. "Let them rob us blind if they want to. You are way more important than the crap in this house."

A determined look crossed Sasha's face as she stared Charles down. Paulie could tell she was about to force the issue. The woman was as stubborn as they came, and she didn't like the word 'no'. Paulie almost smiled. They could be siblings for how alike they were.

"Stay put," Paulie told her. "I'll go flush him out. I'll call for help if I think they are likely to kill me."

Her flat stare swung his way. Paulie could see the indecision. The desire to sprint into the battle. He also saw a shadow of vulnerability that made his stomach clench. He didn't know her that well, but she'd given him a chance when everyone else his whole life turned their backs on him. He'd do a helluva lot more than just run around a house to keep her safe. She was blood now.

Her hand lightly rested on the bump of her stomach. "Okay," she said quietly.

"A few more months and then you can storm the enemy." Paulie gave her a wink. "Now, where am I headed and am I allowed to kill?"

"He's gone." Stefan glanced around at his Guard. They'd all but surrounded the shifter in stealth, but when they moved in for the capture, it took off. "He's good. I'd bet he's done this more than a few times."

"Good at evading capture, yes. We've had the same problem." Tim stood beside them in sweat pants and a surly expression. "He's not interested in me. He catalogued my operation and hasn't come back. Now it's your turn."

"Who is a strange shifter reporting to if not more

shifters?" Jameson asked as he turned back toward the Mansion.

"That's the question, isn't it?" Stefan growled as he followed him. They shouldn't have this much of a problem with a single shifter. It had a scent, its magic had a scent—finding it and destroying it should be ten times easier than dealing with one of Andris' schemes. So why couldn't they lock him down?

Then it occurred to him. Sasha. She was largely off duty. Had she been able to amble through the city, as she did, with Charles and Jonas at her back, she would've found this shifter by now. She would've felt its magic, used her sixth sense, and led them all right to it. Then Stefan would've moved in with his forces and snatched the thing up. So easy. When working with her, everything became so easy.

He was largely off duty, too and yet he had to admit he hadn't ventured too far because he'd wanted her close and wouldn't lead her into any sort of danger. He couldn't help it. She was on his mind constantly. More than ever before. Even though she was safely locked inside the Mansion, he felt panic creeping into him that he wasn't with her. Their life was on hold for this baby, and he couldn't say he was really beat up about one shifter running around loose.

The implications of there being something larger behind that one shifter, though...

Stefan's phone buzzed in his pocket. He fished it out and saw a text from Charles, "Shifter out front. One got inside. Paulie checking it out."

"There's more," Stefan said, a blast of panic stealing his breath. "One's inside the Mansion."

Everyone sprung to life. Stefan sprinted ahead with Tim right at his side.

"What kind of shifter? What's he after?" Tim asked, ripping off his shirt.

"Charles didn't say. Paulie, the human, is going after it. He's good in a brawl, but he doesn't have control over his magic."

"Any shifter, no matter how untrained, will rip him apart." Tim stalled to slip out of his sweats. A moment later, a blast of magic saw a human change into a huge Kodiak bear. It didn't take long for the bear to catch up with Stefan's guards, and even less time for it to easily overtake them.

"He lumbers along and you think he's barely moving," Jameson said through his rapid breathing. "Look at his speed, though."

Wolves and a mountain lion weren't far behind, the shifters easily faster than anything with two legs. Stefan and his crew put on a burst of speed, but they were still going to be showing up late to the party. Stefan only hoped Sasha knew to stay put.

∿

PAULIE INCHED INTO THE DESERTED HALLWAY. HE'D SEEN the Watch run through a while ago. They were probably headed to fortify the front and other entrances. Charles had clearly let the Boss know about the additional shifters. That wouldn't stop the intruder, though. Someone was already inside checking things out. Trying to figure out what the deal with these people was, probably.

He glanced into a room off the hallway. It held a few couches and chairs and a bunch of silent clan members. These were the non-essential crowd, instructed to get the hell out of the way and stay quiet so the Watch could work. They were dressed and ready for battle. Each held a dagger or a sword, and all had watchful expressions. Their gazes tracked him as he stalked by.

One room down, a million to go.

Sasha had said the shifter changed near the back of the Mansion, then went into an area close to the strategy room. Paulie was about ten feet away from that, now.

He stalked up to the strategy room and halted beside the half closed door. I'll be damned. She was right.

This door was usually either wide open, or totally closed. There were no half measures where this room was concerned. Someone was using it, or not. No one was allowed in here but a select few, and when they discussed business, they didn't do it so others could hear.

Paulie peered through but could only see the end of the long table where a small portion of the territory map was visible.

The territory map. That made sense. The Boss was not one to fuck with, so he should be one to steer clear of. Staying just outside the territory would accomplish that. Then watch and wait in case any sort of opportunity presented itself.

Paulie wanted to meet whoever was in charge. He knew what the hell he was doing. Very smart.

Paulie stepped directly in front of the door, gathered his magic, and kicked. The bang sent the door tearing open. It slapped against the wall. A blond man in his mid-thirties startled. His gaze snapped up to Paulie.

"What the fuck are you doing in here?" Paulie asked in his deep rasp. His sword lit up a deep orange. He couldn't quite pull more to push into gold. It would have to do.

"What are you? Are you human?" the man asked with disdain. "They let you filth run around?"

"I'm half, and you're an idiot, being that you're human, too, dumb-shit." Paulie put just enough spite in his voice to make it sound like that was a sore subject. Might as well let them keep their inaccurate information.

The shifter, completely nude, edged toward the window. His gaze took in the sword, and Paulie's stance. The man grinned. "Half, huh? And reminded of it constantly. Don't know much about that sword…"

"I know enough. For example, I know that if I stick this pointy end in your soft parts, you won't like it much."

With a blast of greenish magic, the flesh of the man melted. Black fur sprouted as teeth turned into canines and nails turned into claws. A large black dog with yellow eyes now stood in the corner of the room.

"A dog, huh? Jesus—a little low on that totem pole yourself. Not even a wolf, or a dingo—you're a damn dog." Paulie stepped closer with a swagger. In a few more feet he'd rush the animal. He could probably try a spell, but he had that same problem Sasha had experienced when she first started—he kept using the inverted spells and blowing things up. He didn't think killing this bugger was the best approach. They needed info. A flesh wound and bindings—he'd done that a million times in his old life.

Although…on humans. Not dogs.

The dog's lips pulled away from his gums in a silent snarl. He did not like the taunting.

"I bet you wait to bed a woman before you tell her what you turn into, huh? Try to get her liking your inner beauty before you have to break the news?" Paulie laughed and took two more steps.

The animal began a low growl. It stepped toward the end of the table with a clear shot of the door. Paulie stepped in the same direction, blocking its path. This thing would charge, and Paulie would act. Any time now. This was about to go down—

A loud and low snuffle sounded off right behind him. Paulie jumped and backed to one side so both whatever had just come in the door and the dog were still in sight. He then nearly crapped his pants.

A huge bear—probably Tim because there couldn't be

more than one massive bear in this area-- was standing in the doorway. Twice as big as a normal bear, this thing was a huge boulder of muscle and power. Only one thought ran through Paulie's head: I'm not the top of the food chain, anymore.

The dog must've thought the same thing. It let loose a whimper and started running for the door. The bear gave a grunt and took a hop-step toward the window. The dog, in what must've been blind panic, changed his path and jumped straight at the window. Shards of glass rained down as the window broke and allowed the animal through.

The bear roared. The sound shook the walls and almost stopped Paulie's heart. The huge animal ran at the window, but there was no way it could fit through. It would have to take down the wall, and that was doubtful.

Paulie could, though.

Summoning his magic and doing exactly what Master Bert had incorrectly shown him, Paulie threw a spell to create a warming orb. When the spell hit the wall, the whole place erupted. Chunks of wall blasted outward. The explosion rocked the Mansion. A huge hole opened up in the side of the strategy room.

With another grunt, and without waiting for the smoke to clear, the bear took off in pursuit. He didn't have far to go, though. A collection of wolves and a mountain lion waited on the other side, surrounding a cage made of burnished gold magic. Inside the cage was a black dog and a puddle of blood.

"He must've cut himself on the window!" Paulie yelled as he ran through the wall after the bear. "Stitch him up quick or he can't tell us who his employers are!"

A Watch member ran forward. A blast of magic had the bear turning into Tim, panting and kneeling. He rose slowly, as if he'd just run three miles, and stepped closer to the dog. The box winked out as he approached.

"It wouldn't matter," Tim said with disgust. "This is way too much blood, and this shifter isn't even trying to make it."

"It's his throat." One of the Watch, a woman with auburn hair, knelt down and pointed at the glistening neck. "Yeah, he's a goner."

"Turn back to human," Stefan said as he also knelt beside the form.

"Push on a wound to coax an answer," someone instructed.

The woman reached for a blood coated furry shoulder but it was too late. With a low whimper, the rising and falling of the dog's chest stopped.

"Shit." Stefan stood and looked into the room. His gaze hit Paulie next. "Is she safe? She didn't chase this guy?"

"No. I came instead. Boss, listen, this guy wasn't in the map room by accident. I'd bet these guys are trying to get the perimeter of your territory down. That's what I'd do. You're too strong to take without heavy losses, so the best bet is to stick to the outskirts and watch. Don't broach the territory until you are ready to make a move. It's the smartest play."

"And how do you figure all that?" Tim asked with a furrowed brow.

"He spent some time on the street," Stefan answered for him. "He was one of the go-to guys for his gang. It was a mid-level gang without a lot of clout, but under this human's guidance, they held more territory than a lot of larger gangs. In prison, he was rarely messed with. And those who did didn't walk away. He's never been accused of playing someone dirty —he seems to have a strong sense of loyalty."

Paulie couldn't help his wide eyes and the uncomfortable urge to get the hell out of that black-eyed stare.

"I did some checking up on you. I can't have an unknown around my mate." Stefan walked into the Mansion. "It bears some looking into, but without knowing who's running the show, we're at a dead end. I'll talk to Cato and Dominicous— see what they've heard. We need that panther, though. He is the one with the answers."

Paulie noticed Selene standing off to the side. Her eyes were hungry and beauty ethereal. But he wasn't in the mood. Without another glance at anyone, he made his way back to his room. He couldn't shake a strange, warm feeling.

The Boss had checked up on him. He had learned of all of Paulie's past failings. He had found out about the time he had done in prison, the gruesome fights that he'd been in, and his resolve to not be bothered. He'd been vicious and nasty in prison in the beginning—it had been the only way to ensure people left him alone. And on the street he had horror story after horror story. The Boss knew about all of that too, and still he'd let Paulie guard his pregnant wife. He'd trusted Paulie with his most precious thing in the world.

Paulie wiped his face as he ducked into his room on the second floor. The leader of these people—the hard ass who could control a guy with one look—believed in him. Sasha, the intelligent mage on top of the world, believed in him. They didn't think he was trash or garbage. For the first time in his life, two people had looked past his mistakes and saw the man underneath.

He'd already given them his loyalty, but now he'd give his life if it meant those two people could keep breathing. He'd work his ass off to be worthy of this clan. And he'd find that panther. He still had a few favors he could call in. More than anyone else, he knew how this shit worked. He was their best bet, and he'd prove it.

CHAPTER NINE

"*I* am so sick of being pregnant!" I finished off my statement with an anguish-filled groan.

I'd been at this for eight months and one week. Except for that incident four or so months before, that shifter and his friends had taken off again. No one could figure out what the hell they wanted. Why have a look around and then keep disappearing for long stretches? It didn't make any sense.

Obviously, this was all good news for me. Great timing, actually. I let the Watch hem and haw and strategize while I continued being pregnant and staring out the window.

The first three months had been fraught with morning sickness. That sucked, but I got over it. The middle three were bliss, except for that little situation with the breaking-and-entering shifters. The final trimester, though...that wasn't much fun. For me, anyway. Stefan couldn't be happier. He got to feel the babies move without peeing every five minutes, or being extremely uncomfortable, or not being able to sleep.

Yes. Babies. Plural. I was having two. At one time.

Like I said, the disappearing shifter was great news for me. I had enough on my plate as it was.

Having twins was unheard of with Stefan's race, they had said. And they had said it, over and over. So now I was a poster child for procreation. If I didn't win their hearts with my magic and saving their leader, this would've done it. I was a celebrity.

A very, very grumpy and uncomfortable celebrity. Hooray.

"Almost there, beautiful. Just a few more weeks." Stefan held my hand as we walked down the hallway of the Mansion.

People didn't crowd in, anymore. They knew better.

"Good evening, almost parents," Charles said with a smile as he walked up. Paulie followed behind. "Ready?"

"We're taking it easy as we head to the Farm." Stefan gave my hand an encouraging squeeze.

Charles put a hand on my belly.

The next second Charles was airborne. He slammed against the wall and slid down into a heap. "Damn it, Sasha! That's not how a new mother is supposed to react to people sharing the gift of life with her!"

"That's how a human mother reacts." Paulie smirked.

"Charles, I told you I didn't want to be touched anymore. I told everyone. Why is it you are the only one who doesn't learn?"

"Because he hasn't figured out how to reverse the blood flow from his dick back to his head." Jonas was waiting by the wall ten feet in front of us.

"You talk about my dick a lot, bro. I'm totally cool if you want to get on your knees and praise it." Charles picked himself off the ground.

Jonas was in the best mood I'd ever seen him. I think it was because I was so surly, and had zapped Charles several times, that he figured he could take over my previous happiness. Whatever rocked his concert. Just as long as he let me keep being surly. It helped me cope a little.

As soon as we reached him, he pushed off the wall and

kept pace. He glanced at Paulie, who always walked a little behind us. My newest bodyguard seemed more comfortable being just that little bit removed.

"Human male, have you heard anything from your contacts?" Jonas asked, letting some of his growl seep back into his voice.

"That shifter ain't been around. There's been no strange goings-on in the human world. Nothing. In fact, things seem quiet. Maybe a little too quiet."

"Dun dun dunnnnn," I sang. And then I scowled, just because.

In an attempt to find the shifter, Paulie had contacted some of his old "working" buddies. He'd found out that the shifter had left at the north end of the city in a black Mercedes. These connections knew people in the neighboring areas, and that Mercedes hadn't been spotted anywhere. Whoever that guy was, he wasn't local. And, he'd gotten out of town pretty quick.

Since that information had been so helpful, Stefan authorized a payroll. Paulie became the eyes and ears of his previous thug world, but without the illegal activity that would get him involved with the cops. He just gathered information. Since his guys knew him, and as he always paid in cash and still hated the police, it worked just fine. Nobody minded giving seemingly random information about nobodies.

"You going to stay with her, Boss?" Charles asked. He'd picked up his position right next to me. Soon he'd reach for my belly, unable to help himself, and I'd blast him again. It was like a song on auto-repeat.

"I'll sleep there, but I need to hit a few meetings here during the day time just to make sure everything keeps running smoothly." My hand got another squeeze. "Just a couple hours out of the day."

Tears sprang to my eyes unbidden. I was terrified of him leaving me. Absolutely terrified. I couldn't even think of it without crying. It felt like my lifeline was being ripped away.

The clan doctor said that was a normal reaction for a heavily pregnant female. That when I was at the farm, they would try and comfort the part of me that craved my mate's company. The human midwife had patted my hand and said I'd be fine. She thought it was hormones.

I didn't know what it was, but I was uncomfortable, my ankles were the size of my upper arms, I was short of breath, I still had to pee even though I just freaking peed, and I wanted to cry and punch things, simultaneously.

"I just want this to be over," I whined.

"Walking helps," Paulie said quietly. "Get your man to rub your feet."

We reached the back of the Mansion to be greeted by a small crowd. Everyone was smiling with sparkling eyes. Some had a tear or two. "Good luck!" many said. One guy opened the door for my entourage. "Good luck!"

Ann waited for us outside, the flare of her blue hair lost to the darkness. "Ready?"

She'd be coming with me. Like luggage. It was acknowledged that I would need a female that I knew well to help me relax. Delilah said she'd go, which was great, but I wanted Ann, too. And when I'd called Tim asking about it, I'd received an easy yes. Why? Because I threatened his life, obviously.

And then threatened it again when he started laughing at me.

Whatever. I got my way.

"How's those kids? Moving?" Ann asked as she shoved Charles out of the way so she could be at my side.

"Real nice." Charles tried to crowd in behind. The guy was probably just as excited as Stefan. Jonas was too, but he did a better job of hiding it beneath his, "I hate everyone" exterior.

"Going quiet, now," I answered. "They're turned down and dropping and all that. Wanting to come out. I want them to come out."

"Twins usually come early, right?" She put a hand on my shoulder to slow me down as Jonas walked ahead quickly to get the door.

"That's what they say. Any time. Twins, Ann! Why me?"

"We're blessed, that's why," Stefan said with soft eyes. "Almost there, baby. And then I can help."

"Oh, you better help. You better bust your ass. You have a lot to make up for, mister!" I grumbled.

My romantic streak was long gone. Long, long gone.

Stefan lifted me into the backseat of Jonas' Hummer. It was both awkward, and a whole lot of weight, but he bore it easily. I scowled at the seat, just because. He got in the other side so he could sit next to me. Charles and Jonas got in the front with Ann sandwiched in the middle of them. Paulie crawled in the back so as not to crowd Stefan. He'd be coming back for class, but said he wanted to drop me off.

I really wished this car ride meant labor. If only hopes were miracles.

FORTY-FIVE MINUTES LATER, WE PULLED OFF THE HIGHWAY onto a small dirt road. At the end of that was an arch above a gate that said, "Triple-T Farm."

"I feel like a cow," I muttered as Jonas reached out the window and entered a code. The gate shuddered to a start before slowly swinging open.

"You're almost there," Ann noted.

I was tired of people saying that. But then, I was tired of most things, so I didn't say anything.

We wound through trees and uncultivated grass until we approached a smallish cabin nestled into the trees. Jonas parked right out in front and the whole progression emptied the car, me being last. By the time we were organized in a tighter than necessary horde, I noticed a woman dressed all in pink. Beside her stood a moderately large Delilah with a huge smile, and Delilah's man, Tom, standing beside her with a hand on her back.

"Finally you come out here!" Delilah exclaimed. "You are going to kick yourself for not being here sooner. This is the most relaxing place."

"Nowhere is a relaxing place," I grumbled.

"Hello, Sasha. I'm Genevieve. Delilah, why don't you show her around? Let her walk a little. With her size, that car must've been cramped." Genevieve smiled at me in commiseration. I liked her already.

"Boss," the woman turned her attention to Stefan. "If you plan to leave, why don't you walk her around first and get her settled in her room. That would be the best for her stress levels."

"Of course," Stefan said meekly.

Ann and I were the only people to turn and stare at him with a slack jaw. Apparently his rank meant little in this place. Delilah smiled harder.

"C'mon," Delilah said, starting forward. Tom followed her like a shadow.

She led us through the trees to a flat and totally level dirt path. There were no snags, roots, or rocks to catch the feet. On the side was even a railing to hold onto.

"So, this whole place is set up for pregnant people?" I asked in awe.

"Not really. You'll see."

"I can't believe you've never been out here," Ann noticed. "Isn't that one of the first things you should do when taking over a job? Figure out the stuff you're protecting."

"Ann, I am not in the mood for a critic." That was a better thing to say then, "Yup. My bad."

Through the trees we emerged into a clear-cut area large enough for a football game. Neat rows of garden covered every inch.

"Oh! This is what the cooks were always talking about when they said they were giving me the best crops. I wondered, but they always gave me a weird grin and said I'd see."

"And now you see." Delilah laughed and led the way along the path, not bothering to go into the garden.

Next we saw another grassy area where cows and other livestock were held. They weren't in great supply, but I noticed a dairy area and equipment I thought was for making butter. And this was why everything tasted so fresh. I'd thought we'd spent an arm and a leg on organic produce, but it seemed we made it ourselves.

I had been so preoccupied with learning my mage duties I hadn't properly looked into how the Mansion ran. It was a glaring black mark on my job as co-leader.

"I didn't take up all the operations right away, either," Stefan said in an encouraging tone. "People at the Mansion grow up with all this, so we know most things going into a leadership role. Now that you are underway with your mage duties, I'll start involving you in all this. It'll help to share some of the duties."

"Did you not pick up any of these tidbits when you were sitting in on all those meetings?" Ann asked. A grin peeked through her shock. She knew the answer, the jerk.

"Daydreaming," I mumbled.

My hand got a squeeze.

Halfway through the tour my body started to ache. As

soon as I visibly flagged, Delilah turned back toward the main house.

"I almost don't want to get to your stage," Delilah muttered. Tom rubbed her back.

"You're telling me," Ann burst out. "If I want a baby, it's going to be born in a test tube."

"You plan to live for another thousand years?" Charles badgered.

"If I need to."

"Nope, won't work. I want one sooner."

Ann turned to Charles with an incredulous expression. "Is that right?"

"No fighting," Delilah chastised. "You're around pregnant people."

Charles immediately humbled. Ann continued to stare.

We filed into the main house and found Genevieve sitting behind a computer. She stood immediately and motioned us to follow her. "We are putting you in the largest suite so as to accommodate all the visitors I anticipate you getting. You said Council member Dominicous and his mage Toa will be joining us, correct?"

"Yes. They will be arriving shortly," Stefan answered.

"And of course the human magic workers." Genevieve led us through a backdoor. A large facility, separated from the small main house, stretched out in front of us. Three stories and housing a whole lot of rooms, this place was as big as a hospital.

We entered the building. Plush carpet and beautiful window dressings greeted us. A sitting area held overstuffed couches and a sea of pillows while a refreshment stand was stocked with snacks and drinks and a small refrigerator.

"Jeez. This is like a five-star resort and a hospital combined into one."

"When can I move in," Paulie mumbled with wide eyes.

Two people on the couches turned awkwardly to look our way. I didn't recognize them, but they said, "Welcome Mage," immediately. Then, "Congratulations, Boss."

"Hey, Charlene. You got a mate yet, or what?" Charles called.

"Haven't chosen yet. Might leave my options open. Why, you asking?" a pretty woman with deep red hair asked.

"We'll see if I can steal the Boss' girl," Charles retorted.

"I'll bring flowers to your funeral!" The two women cackled.

"She's insane," Charles muttered to Jonas as we started to walk. "Too crazy for even you, bro. Baby or no, there is no way."

Jonas snorted. "I gave her a try a while ago. She didn't hold up and then started bitching about what a freak I was."

"Bro, everyone knows you're a freak. What was her deal?" Charles shook his head with a put-upon expression.

"That's what I asked her. She tried to stab me."

"Can you guys share your twisted sex lives another time?" I asked.

"Ditto that question," Ann said.

I followed the others as we went down a hallway. Genevieve led us to a door at the very end. She stepped aside so Stefan and I could go in first. The room was huge with a waiting room in the front housing two couches, a loveseat and three recliners. Another refreshment stand was set up at the far wall, along with a phone and a bell. Through a door in the back was a large, four-poster bed dressed with down. I had a closet full of fuzzy robes and sweats, and a huge bathroom with a large bathtub and more refreshments.

I thought living with Stefan was luxury, but this was in another league all together. The Ritz would be hard-pressed to compete with this suite.

"Okay, love, I'm going to go take care of some things, then I'll meet you back here." Stefan leaned down to kiss me.

My heart started beating wildly. I clutched on to his hand unable to help myself, feeling a huge chasm of the unknown opening up around me. "Are you sure?" I asked. Tears came to my eyes.

"I do this whenever Tom tries to leave, too," Delilah said softly. It sounded like she was talking to someone else, but I didn't look over to find out who. I just stared at Stefan's handsome face and willed him to stay with me.

"I'll try to hurry everyone up," Stefan said softly, putting his forehead to mine. "I'll be back before you know it."

"Okay," I whispered.

He gave me one last, deep kiss before he stepped away. I pried my hand from his, already feeling hollow.

"The strength of the bond of mating grows during the pregnancy," Genevieve said in a serene voice. "This must've developed over hundreds of years of mates being unsure of biological parents. The female taking the male's blood creates a sort of need in the male to protect at all costs. He is more thoroughly attached than human males with their pregnant wives. Sharing blood creates the need and willingness to be governed and protected in the females. This bond is something that forms extremely tight-knit families. It's truly remarkable."

Ann shifted her weight to her right leg and put her hand on her hip. "Say I got knocked up by one of these guys, right?"

"Like me," Charles threw in.

Ann rolled her eyes at his cheesy smile. "You're saying I'd suddenly want to suck blood?"

Genevieve smiled at her. "If you hadn't already, probably not. But if you tried it during your pregnancy, you'd probably find you quite liked it. And your body would easily accept it during the pregnancy."

"I couldn't before I was pregnant—it really killed my stomach. But I can now," Delilah said. "I like it."

"Gross." Ann shivered.

"Let's get the show on the road," Jonas growled. "This is causing Sasha unneeded stress."

"He's right, love." Stefan kissed me again. He steered Jonas toward me. Jonas reached out and took my hand as if it was a completely normal thing for him to do. "He'll guard you in my absence, okay?"

"Why does this feel normal?" I asked, blinking up at Jonas. "You're holding my hand."

"It is such a treat to witness humans interacting with our race in this way," Genevieve said with a laugh. "They crave the things we take for granted, and then marvel at them. It is quite a behavior study. Some things are more deeply ingrained in our primal needs than I had realized."

For some reason I couldn't explain, I wanted to punch her. Delilah started to laugh—I must've advertised that thought on my face.

Stefan gave me a sorrowful wink before leaving. I squeezed Jonas' hand tightly, and then reached for Charles'. It felt like my heart was leaving with Stefan, like I'd never see him again.

CHAPTER TEN

*S*tefan shut the car door and paused for a moment. He let out a breath and closed his eyes against the guilt of leaving her. He knew it was irrational, but the pounding ache of wanting to go back inside was hard to fight.

"You okay, Boss?" Paulie asked as he stared straight ahead. "Need a minute?"

"No. I'm good."

Stefan started the car and tried to clear his thoughts. He tried to focus on driving back to the Mansion, getting his stuff done, and returning as fast as possible.

"She's got some mean bastards with her. And she's got magic way beyond anyone in the Mansion. She'll be good for a couple hours," Paulie said.

"Yeah." Stefan stepped on the gas.

"If they need a car, though..."

"There are vehicles here if they need one." Stefan took the corner too fast and forced himself to slow down. It wouldn't help if he killed himself in his urgency to get back to her.

"So it's a trip, huh? Your people seem to think it's like Christmas knowing you sired a kid."

Stefan glanced at the male next to him who hadn't said more than a handful of words to him in the last nine months. "What?"

Paulie continued to stare straight ahead, completely relaxed. "Huge deal for your kind to know it's your kid. Kind of a trip, huh?"

"Are you trying to distract me?"

"Yeah. Working?"

Stefan's lips quirked as he turned onto a main road. Surprisingly, it was. "It is a trip, yes. I hear it's made you in demand. The durability of human procreation, I mean."

"Oh yeah. I don't get any blowjobs, though. Except from Selene. They all want the baby maker. I actually got kicked in the face when I tried to use protection. I don't know if I want a bunch of kids I created running around. In human land, that would be seriously complicated."

Stefan couldn't help a smile. "Hasn't stopped you any."

"Ah...no. You got some hot women and Selene is cool with an open relationship—I guess most of you are. Kind of a waste to say no, know what I mean?"

Stefan glanced at the human male again. He had no idea that Paulie had a sense of humor. Or any real personality. The male could be good to hang around with. Relaxed and easy, happy to let the small things go.

Stefan didn't know why he was surprised. Anyone who Sasha welcomed into her inner circle were often extraordinary in some way, and could always banter. Still, it was a nice surprise. It kept things interesting.

They turned into the Mansion ten minutes later and he clicked back on his serious Boss' mask. Jameson was waiting as Stefan got out of the car.

"Everything go okay?" Jameson asked.

"She's good. Let's get moving, though. I need to get back."

"Understood."

PAULIE SQUEEZED HIS EYES SHUT AND FOCUSED ON THE LINK with Birdie. They were the two highest power workers and also the most volatile. Links were fine when Sasha was in control because she could easily manage the vast quantities of magic. Without her as the pinnacle, though, it was not so easy.

"Stop pulling!" Birdie huffed with a red face. "You're not supposed to bash people around when you call the corners. You're supposed to join everyone else. This is why guys get kicked out of the sisterhood."

"This ain't why. Having a penis is why. Guys don't want to listen to your nonsense." Paulie took a deep breath and tried to still his mind. Tried to just be with the increased flow of magic battering at his senses. This much power was no joke. If you didn't constantly keep yourself in some sort of chi, it would crash down on top of you and roll you over. Paulie hadn't survived his life this far to get steamrolled by a freaking fairy tale.

He and Birdie sat in Master Bert's class on the top floor of the Mansion among a bunch of pubescents. They were in an advanced class that was currently focusing on spell casts, charms, and linking. All the kids could already do it reasonably well. It was the humans who were struggling. Without Sasha they were mostly hopeless.

The breeding program that Birdie and Delilah were instigating sounded less and less asinine.

"Okay, do a spell." Birdie sat in a chair in front of him with her fingers curled tightly around the arms. She was the only one to get a seat. While she could get up off the floor, no one wanted to chance her not being able to. The cold did something to her bones, or some shit, and she got terribly cranky when she was still.

Even Master Bert was wary.

"Maw, how is everyone doing?" Master Bert threaded his way through the focusing students. "If you have the link stabilized, try a spell. Maw, that is the next step."

"God, that guy is creepy." Paulie put out his hands to give the illusion of balance. Eyes still squeezed shut, he focused all his attention on weaving a spell for a small plant. Just a little green thing that might grow out of the pot of dirt between him and Birdie. Nothing big. Should be easy.

"Don't you create a monster," Birdie warned. Sweat dribbled down her cheeks. "Do not invert that spell!"

He didn't need to be told. The classroom had just been patched up from his last spell-gone-wild.

He worked the elements with a smooth and delicate hand. He tried to do as Birdie said and be at one with her. Tried to grow a vagina and hang with the gals. Tried to bend the spell just right, and then he could gently, ever so gently, lay—

His phone screamed from his pocket.

He jumped. His spell curled and then wobbled. The elements clashed.

"Oh shi—" A zing of power blasted out in all directions. Firecracker-like magic zipped through the class, burning anyone it crashed against.

"Damn it, human!" one of the kids yelled. People hopped up. Some started to run and wave their hands wildly. Paulie couldn't help chuckling.

"Shield class," Master Bert instructed in a loud voice. "Maw, shielding will protect you from spells such as that. Mostly. They are high in power, but it will singe less."

Paulie's phone trilled again. He fished it out to glares. "Paulie."

"That Mercedes just blew through, man," a gruff voice sounded in the phone.

A cold shiver trickled down Paulie's back. They'd just returned. It'd be another couple of hours before they'd be heading back up to that plush birthing place. Right now, Sasha only had Jonas, Charles and Ann to watch out for her.

"You get a tail on it?" Paulie asked, standing up and waving away Master Bert's irritation with the phone call.

"Yeah. Stopped up near Hyde Park. Met some other guys. They was talking about humans and science and some shit. Something about some human link or something. I think they want into this territory, though. There was talk about clearing out some mage or something—I didn't get that, really. But then some leader. They was talking about the biggest threats and what not. Dangerous, though. They talkin' crazy, but they're dangerous. No guns that I saw, but these guys were carrying some muscle, know what I'm sayin'? I'd wait to get them in an alley with firepower if I was you. Take them out handy-like and then disappear. That's the way to play those guys."

Paulie was out of the classroom and jogging toward the stairs. "Where'd they go after?"

"Headed out of town. A few of 'em. Three white guys with lots of money. Talked like a bunch o' uppity bastards. This ain't no street game, you know that. These fuckers got some clout. All's I'm sayin'. Take 'em out quiet-like and disappear. Safest way to play it. Hold your turf, but you don't gotta advertise which way the wind is blowin', know what I'm sayin'?"

"All right, Rudy. Thanks, man."

"No sweat. Good luck. You need guns for hire, you know who to call."

Paulie didn't need guns for hire. He just needed to point out the danger and let this swarm of vicious, bloodthirsty people kill everything in sight. It was comforting knowing he wasn't the most violent in the crew, anymore. Grounding.

Exhilarating.

Paulie burst into a large meeting room and sought the Boss' eyes immediately. He braced himself against the blast of strength and power in that dark gaze before saying, "That shifter is in town."

The entire room stood in a rush. The Boss was running towards him in the next second, Jameson and three others directly behind.

"What do you know?" the Boss asked as they moved down the hall quickly. People scattered to the sides and held perfectly still for the procession to pass.

Paulie did a quick summary of the phone call. Then said, "They don't want you. Not yet. I don't know who's in charge, but right now they are after the one with the most power— Sasha. Will she defend herself? Will she do what needs to be done if she has to?"

He couldn't imagine her killing anyone. She was such a sweetie. Always putting people before herself, and trying to help everyone out with the magic and fitting in and just getting along. She was more saintly than vigilante.

Everyone chuckled at his question.

"She'll set the world on fire if she has to." The Boss sobered as they burst outside. Jonas' Hummer waited for them in the parking space. The Boss jogged around it as he said, "But she's heavily pregnant. She doesn't have the ability to move much."

Paulie could hear the blind fear in the Boss' voice. It was probably the only time this man would show it.

Jameson stopped beside a blue SUV and pulled open the door. Three people hovered around it as others found their own vehicles. The Boss kept going until he ducked into a covered area at the very far end of the lot. He yanked off a cover and exposed a cherry red Ferrari.

"Holy—" Paulie's mouth dropped open as he slowed.

The Boss glanced his way. "C'mon. Hurry up or you'll be left behind."

"Why haven't I seen this before?"

"It draws attention. But it goes fast. We need speed right now."

"Yes." Paulie couldn't help a grin as he pulled open the door and slid into the plush interior.

As the engine roared into life the Boss said, "Do not tell Sasha about this car. I haven't driven it since she came to live here. She'd steal it and probably kill herself."

"She's going to find out," Paulie muttered.

I STOPPED ALONG THE PATH AND TOOK A MOMENT TO breathe. The fresh breeze tickled my skin and calmed my nerves. The grasses swayed beside me, natural and beautiful. I was no more than fifty yards from the house and definitely ready to head back in. Walking was just a pain in the butt these days. I was tired almost immediately.

But if walking sped this whole pregnancy deal along, it was worth panting over.

Jonas stood beside me, my hand still in his. He wasn't a touchy-feely kinda guy, but when he gave himself to a job, he went whole-hog. It wasn't really helping, though. I wanted Stefan. I wanted his protection and possessiveness. I needed his presence and his assurance that everything would work out okay. That it wouldn't hurt too much.

"Oh, God, this is totally going to hurt, isn't it? And there are two," I whined.

I felt the squeeze of Jonas' hand. "It'll be okay. You won't even feel the second."

"Seriously, Jonas?"

I got a grunt. Yeah, that was a dumb thing to say.

I glanced up and saw that Charles and Ann were descending the path to us. They'd stayed behind to get food setup even though there were staff on duty around the clock. I had a feeling Charles didn't trust them to put out enough food for him. The man ate more than two people combined.

I stopped for a moment and closed my eyes to feel the breeze. I took a few breaths. And then felt Jonas tense beside me.

I opened my eyes and saw Ann and Charles on the path up ahead. They were both looking out over the field.

Like a gunshot blast, I felt it. My gaze swung out over the mostly fallow field covered in long grasses.

"I'm supposed to be safe here," I muttered with a tingle working up my spine.

I took stock magically, identifying location, my gaze slid across a pair of eyes. I picked up that familiar feeling. The shifter! Two yellow eyes from a predator at the top of the food chain stared at me before the world burst into movement. A feline body was in the air, claws spread wide and jaw opened. Jonas stepped in front of me to take the attack as his sword arched outwards.

He wouldn't be able to bring it up in time.

It didn't matter. I'd reacted without even meaning to.

Power pulsed and pounded around me. A wall of electric razors zigzagged in front of Jonas and I. It sliced into the furry body before a solid wall of magic slammed into the body from the side. The panther screamed as it was pushed to the side. Its body hit the ground and rolled, smears of red coating the ground behind it.

Jonas was on it a moment later, sword out, ready for a kill strike.

"No!" I screamed. I threw a cage around it and then a shock barrier to keep Jonas away. "We need info from that asshole. What the hell is he doing following me? Where does he go when he's not loitering around town? And in what screwed up world is it okay to try and kill a heavily pregnant woman? What the hell is wrong with that guy?"

"Oh, shit, we shouldn't have killed them?"

I glanced from a seething Jonas and the whimpering panther to see Charles with a mountain lion standing next to him. Both had blood splatters across them and two bodies at their feet. One was a lioness, the other a lynx.

"All cats," I said softly. "To sneak around, I guess. What the hell were they planning?"

I glanced back at the panther as a hard stab of pain rocked my body. I put a hand to my stomach and reached for Jonas. "Ow."

"What's happening?" Charles jumped over the bodies and sprinted down the path.

Jonas took my hand and put his arm behind my back.

"Let's go back." I didn't hurt at the moment, but I was in the absence of pain. When this far along in pregnancy, the absence of pain means that it is crouching, just waiting to unleash havoc.

"Is that critter going to die if we leave it?" Jonas asked.

I glanced back at the caged panther. It was still on its side, oozing a small amount of blood and panting. It probably hurt quite a lot, but it wasn't life threatening. "The razor spell wasn't meant to cut deep. It probably went a little deeper than I intended as I was keyed up. Oops. It'll be—"

An overall tightening of my tummy stopped my words. The pain spiraled outwards and radiated up through my body. It wasn't terrible, though. It was just a promise of agony.

"Was that a contraction?" Charles asked with a wildness to his eyes. He squeezed my hand, all thought of the attack and shifters completely forgotten. "Are you starting? It is starting, Sasha? Should I get help? Does it hurt—"

Jonas stepped around me and punched Charles in the face. Charles staggered back. He shook his head. "Thanks, bro. I needed that. I think I just panicked."

A childlike cry pierced the night. Jonas glanced up the path. "Yes, Ann, tell them we're coming. We have lots of time yet, but get them to call the Boss."

"Should we carry her, Jonas?" Charles asked in hasty words. "Crap, I'm totally panicking, bro. I was so excited, and now I'm—"

Jonas sent him a glare cutting him off. Another punch might not be far behind, that was clear.

"Let's walk," I said with determination. "That'll help. Walking helps—both doctors agreed on that."

We got to the front of the large compound after stopping twice. It was as if we hadn't just been attacked. There were bigger things to worry about--the pain was definitely contractions. It was happening. The time had come, and I was terrified of the pain as it increased in ferocity.

Not to worry, Charles was panicking every few minutes and getting punched by Jonas. It kept my mind off the terror at hand.

We heard a rumble of cars toward the front as a naked Ann ran into view. She stopped along the path and turned back to three unhurried women in pink. Fresh as a spring morning, they glided toward me with smiles that could probably bloom roses. I felt relief wash over me. They would know what to do—their complete lack of freaking out was evidence of that fact. Something not even Jonas could manage, if his shaking hand was any judge.

A rev that sounded like a fancy sports car had me slowing

my step. The moon glinted off sleek lines and a shiny surface. It slid to a stop and cut off before Stefan slid out.

"What the hell has he kept from me?" I said in a hushed tone.

"Oh crap. Sasha, no. That is off-limits. You'll kill me in that." Charles tugged me to get me moving. He was punched again by Jonas and then gently moved aside by the helpers in pink.

"Jonas, bro, seriously. You haven't been in the car when she drives crazy. She'd kill herself."

"Let's just wait for the Boss and then we will all go inside," one of the ladies said in a voice as gentle and beautiful as a meadow in summer. She was totally suited for her job.

Stefan jogged up with Paulie at his back. I heard more cars in the distance but couldn't see them yet. When Stefan met my eyes, the tightness around his eyes vanished. The haggard look of fear washed away into relief. He slowed to a walk and held out his hand for Paulie to do the same. They approached like a couple guys out for a stroll.

"Hi, baby. Everything going well?" Stefan asked in a calm voice.

A different sort of relief washed over me. It wasn't of helpers knowing what they were doing, or Charles and Jonas acting like dorks, it was the stability and grounding only Stefan could give me. I entwined my fingers with his and heaved a huge sigh.

"Three shifters. Tried to attack her, and in the state she's in." The vicious growl bespoke horrible torture that panther would receive if Jonas got his way. Or any of the clan, really. Probably any species alive, actually. In what world did someone try to kill a pregnant lady? It was a level of disgusting I still couldn't picture.

"Ann and I took two out before Sasha said to keep them alive, though," Charles admitted, his gaze on my face. Then my stomach. "Okay, what are we waiting for? Inside, right, Sasha? We should go inside?"

"You kept one alive?" Stefan asked like he might've been asking if I'd saved him a piece of apple pie.

"Shifter attacked here?" one of the women in pink asked. Shock and fury warred in her features.

"One is hurt but alive, yes." I scrunched up my face as another contraction grabbed a hold of my body and started digging in claws. It was getting worse. The pain was more consuming now.

"Inside, yes," I panted.

"Is she in labor?" Stefan asked in the same calm voice.

"Yes, Boss. And yes, let's all move inside." Another of the ladies in pink motioned us forward. "Boss, maybe you can have one of your men arriving take care of anything that needs to be done while you focus on your mate. She needs you right now."

"Of course. Jonas, take care of it. Paulie, go with him and fill him in on what you know."

"Yes, Boss," someone said as another wave of pain washed over me. Worse and worse. Here we go.

CHAPTER ELEVEN

*C*harles paced in the front room of the suite. He heard Sasha cry out and had to stop and squeeze his fists against the mortal anguish she was obviously in. "Don't they give drugs anymore, bro?" He started pacing again. "I mean, the movies had drugs."

Jonas sat in the chair, gently rocking. Paulie leaned against the wall by the door. Tim, Ann and Delilah sat on couches. Delilah's man was beside her, holding her hand, trying not to look totally freaked out. He was not pulling it off. When a guy in the field sounded like Sasha, that meant he was dying. He was holding his intestines dying a slow, agonizing death.

Jonas had thrown him against the wall when he asked if Sasha was dying. Then one of the annoying women in pink told him to calm down, that this was all standard practice.

Standard my ass. This shit is shit. That's what it is. Shit.

Swearing, even mentally, should've helped. Why didn't it help?

Another tortured cry came from the inner room. She'd been at this for eight hours. In pain for eight hours, and that was serious pain. World-ending pain. Pain someone didn't come back from.

"How is this normal?" Charles muttered. Pacing.

"Why don't you knit?" Ann offered.

Terrible idea. This called for movement. Fighting. Swords.

"What's the deal with that panther? Can I rough him up or something? Let's get a pen together and I'll fight that bastard. That'd give me something to do." Charles flexed his fingers.

"We have him squared away. We'll question him after Sasha has the babies and Stefan can get away. I'd also like to wait until Dominicous and Toa get—"

A soft knock sounded at the door. A smiling woman in pink— though smiling at a time like this seemed ridiculous— crossed the room and opened the door. Dominicous stepped in with a hopeful expression. Mr. I-Stare-Constantly, Toa, glided in right behind him.

"How is she?" Dominicous asked in a hush. He carried a huge teddy bear under each arm. Toa held a giant bouquet of flowers.

The agonizing scream sounded again. That door didn't do much to muffle the torture of childbirth.

"She's nine centimeters dilated. Won't be too long now." The woman gave that irritating smile again and took the presents. Dominicous smiled, too, as if there wasn't someone in anguish in the next room.

Charles wasn't cut out for this. He wasn't up for this kind of thing.

"Dominicous, we have an issue you might need to know about. I'm not sure how much Stefan has told you," Tim said, his eyes tight. He was trying to act cool, but childbirth was freaking him out, too. Charles could tell.

"Did the panther surface again?" Dominicous asked pleasantly. It was hard to miss the edge to his voice, though.

Toa sat at the opposite end of the couch as Tim. He stared at Charles with those icy blue eyes.

"Not in the mood, bro." Charles paced toward the other side of the room.

"You would think this is your child," Toa said. "You have a deep loyalty toward Sasha, it seems."

"Give that guy a prize, someone. It only took him a couple years to clue into what everyone else already knew."

"The humor, yes. I had forgotten." Toa sniffed and shifted his gaze. Thankfully.

Jonas cracked a smile. Which dwindled at the next cry from the other room.

"He tried to attack Sasha," Paulie said in a growl.

Dominicous turned to the human and took his measure with that flat, assessing stare born of leading men through battles. Paulie held it for a moment, not one to back down from anyone. But, as anyone with a bit of sense did, he looked away not long after. Charles didn't blame him.

"I've heard about you, of course. A human with great potential. Cato can't wait to meet you. You, and a few others Toa is already acquainted with." Dominicous turned back to Tim. "But this attack came...recently?"

"Right before she went into labor," Jonas spoke up. "She was walking in the grounds here and he attacked. His two minions went after Charles and Ann. They were most likely a distraction. The panther must have thought Sasha would be distracted and wouldn't see his attack until too late. He knew she was a mage high in power though."

Dominicous' whole body tensed. His jaw clenched and a vein pulsed in his neck. Burnished gold flared through his tattoos and lit up the blade of his sword attached at his hip.

"Let's just remove all weapons, shall we?" the smiling woman in pink said in an irritatingly pleasant voice.

"He probably didn't think she would be able to do magic

in her advanced state," Toa said thoughtfully. That glacial gaze stared at Jonas.

Jonas stared back with fire. "I think you'll be the best person to get that question answered..."

"Oh yes," Toa agreed before glancing at Dominicous. "I think that is exactly right. Especially if this is someone working with the Europeans. They would've been skeptical of a human being high in power."

"And we don't think he was acting alone?" Dominicous turned to Paulie.

"I have someone tracing his plates. They need to use a hacker I know who's good but expensive," Paulie answered, holding the gaze a little longer that time. "This guy'll come through, though. If there's a trail, he will follow it."

"Useful, this human." Toa turned that eerie gaze on Paulie. Paulie's brows furrowed. "I didn't realize working with a human that had been a criminal could be so advantageous. Sasha does stumble upon some gems."

"Just gotta roll with it, human," Charles muttered. Dealing with Toa could be polarizing. "He's always that weird."

Dominicous was about to speak when the most angelic sound graced their conversation. An infant cry.

"Jonas, if you tell anyone I cried like a bitch, I will kill you in your sleep." Charles wiped his face.

"I would still kick your ass, even asleep, weakling." Jonas' eyes were glassy, too.

Eventually a different baby cry drifted through the door. Still everyone held silent. It wasn't over yet.

Another uncomfortable wait passed before one of the smiling women walked out of the inner room. "Mommy and babies are both fine. A boy and a girl."

Charles could not help the huge smile. Nor the tear dripping down his cheek. The pressure of emotion on his chest was a welcomed one. He couldn't wait to hold one of those squirmy little infants.

~

I WOKE TO SOFTLY FILTERED LIGHT. GENEVIEVE WAS standing beside my bed holding one of my babies. "Time to feed, Sasha," the woman said in a hush.

Stefan climbed out of his side of the bed and came around to take the blue wrapped baby from Genevieve. We'd decided to name him Savion. Genevieve then turned back to her helper for the pink wrapped baby, Sabrina. The tiny little thing was handed down to me.

"Ladies first, Savion." Stefan kissed him on his forehead before staring down at me with an expression dripping love.

It was only a week since having the babies and still my body felt like I'd been through a gruesome battle. I'd been visited by probably everyone in the whole world. Flowers and teddy bears and candy and bottles of wine all littered the suite. Charles and Jonas lingered constantly, always with their hands out to hold the babies. Dominicous and Toa were always first, though.

I was shocked that Toa was totally into kids. Totally into kids. I couldn't remember ever seeing him smile, but when he held Sabrina, his white chompers showed in full force. He played and laughed, bouncing her around the room. Dominicous did the same with Savion

It was clear that my children would never know what it was like to be lonely.

My kids wouldn't grow up like Paulie or me. They wouldn't be awarded to the state with nothing but a "good luck." They wouldn't scratch and fight their way through life, seeing imaginary people and wondering if they were insane. They wouldn't spend every second just surviving. No, they'd be loved and cherished, helped and supported through each stage of their life, regardless of who was looking after them.

That thought had me crying in joy every time I thought of it.

After I had fed Sabrina, I let Stefan take her so I could feed Savion. "How's my beautiful girl?" Stefan said with a smile. He kissed her nose. "You look like your mama."

"Poor thing," I muttered, trying to get Savion to latch. The little guy just wasn't into it. His sister—easy. She took it nearly immediately. He just wouldn't stay on.

"Here, Sasha, let me help." The nurse leaned down to help me.

"Stefan, can you walk her away?" I hated when he watched while I worked at the boobs. It made me feel awkward.

Without a word, he bounced Sabrina toward the window. "Will you like the darkness better, or the light, little girl?" he asked in a soft tone. "Like your mama, or your daddy?"

After I finally got Savion to latch, I watched Stefan with our daughter. He took to parenting within the first moments of Savion's life. He had taken his son and helped wash him while Sabrina was being born. He insisted on holding them both until I was ready. I'd never seen him so happy in my life. He had glossy eyes and a serene expression as he rocked two quiet babies in his arms. As the nurses finished with me, he said, "I love you so much, Sasha. Thank you for giving me the gift of our two beautiful children."

Fate had chosen well with Stefan. I couldn't have picked better myself. Every day I thanked God for him. Every time he kissed me, or kissed our babies, my heart swelled and I felt an answering love through our link. Life was bliss.

CHAPTER TWELVE

*T*wo months after I'd had the babies I was on my way with Jonas and Charles to the shifter compound in the woods. I'd left the babies in the care of two nurses, who would be the kids' nannies. Delilah had been right—there was a huge benefit to having a baby with these people. You got free daycare and nannies. It was a mother's dream.

Which Delilah would know soon enough when she had hers.

"I miss them already," Charles said in a whine. "Sabrina smiled at me, did you see that? Before we left. I think she likes her scarf, even though you won't let her have it."

"That was gas," Jonas growled from the driver's seat.

"You'd smother her with that thing, Charles!" I leaned back and closed my eyes. While there was a day crew to help with feedings, I woke up every time I heard a baby cry. I was hardwired to get all stressed out when it happened. I had help, had a mate that helped, and still I was exhausted. I could not imagine doing it alone.

I hadn't even bothered to ask about the Ferrari everyone

had kept from me. Though now I knew why Stefan never drove himself anywhere.

"That was not gas!" Charles argued. "You're just pissed because Savion scowls at you instead of smiles."

"He's too much like his father," Jonas retorted.

I rolled my eyes.

We pulled to a stop next to Jameson's blue SUV. It was a quiet walk into the main house where they had the shifter tied up in the living room. The marks my spell had left on the guy were long gone, and there were no other marks from Toa except the man's crazy eyes. Charles stayed with me while Jonas ducked out again to ask some shifters if there had been any other sightings. Apparently Tim's guys had smelled people like the clan, but no one had seen anyone. After I had taken a look at the jerk who tried to kill me, I'd go look for some goons trying to hide with their magic. I was no stranger to unraveling an invisibility spell.

The room hushed when I walked in. Tim pushed off the far wall toward me. "Hey Sasha," he said solemnly. "Sorry you had to come here for this."

"I'm ready to go back to work," I said. This jerk tried to kill me right before I gave birth. He had tried to end three lives. I didn't have a soft spot for the guy.

Stefan walked into the room with Paulie right behind him. Stefan gave my back a rub as he passed. "This guy's car is registered to a human in Arizona. Paulie had someone check it out—the humans are long gone. Dead, probably. Their assets are most likely in the hands of this guy's boss. No lead."

The man in the cage stared at the ground. He would not look at me.

I walked directly in front of him and stared down into the physical cage. It was tall enough for him to stand up in and turn around, and wide enough to squat or sit, but not big enough to lie down. That, in itself, was a form of torture.

"So he won't give up what he knows?" I asked with a bite to my words.

The man looked up slowly. He was attractive with light brown eyes and a masculine cleft in his chin. His smile set off warning bells, though. He was cunning and a killer, both. I could see it in the coldness of his eyes.

Not a big deal, though. Everyone in this room was a killer in some form. And this guy would probably see that first hand before long.

"Got yourself in quite the pickle, huh?" I asked in a cheery voice. "Picked on the wrong human."

"Ill planned," he said with a British lilt to his speech. "An issue I will not repeat."

"No. You won't live long enough to. Pity. Right, well, I'll leave Toa to deal with you. I have to go find your clever friends who are probably hiding in the bushes."

The man snorted. "A human with a God complex. How refreshing."

"God complex? Because I can use my magic?" I lightly shook my head. "Never argue with a stupid person, he'll drag you down to his level and then beat you with experience."

I winked at Stefan and made my way outside with Charles following right behind. We checked in with a shifter standing by the door. "Where's Jonas?"

The guy pointed off to the right. I let my magic spread out and walked off that way. Once at the tree line, I glanced way off to the right, and then the left, looking for a grumbling, stocky character. I didn't see one.

"Think he went around the back?" I asked in confusion.

"Doubt it," Charles said, peering into the trees, and then looking back at the house we'd just come out of. "Where'd he go, I wonder."

I pushed my magic as far as I could, feeling the shifters dotting the area but staying away from the house. I walked to the right, trying to push farther. Trying to get a feel of Jonas if nothing else. The guy didn't usually play hide-and-seek.

Halfway to the back I felt something. Up high. A mingling magic and a definite spell working. I glanced up and noticed a branch not quite out straight like its friends, but bent. As if someone was sitting on it. And then I felt the eyes. Very clever.

"Got one," I said quietly.

Charles looked up as I unraveled a pretty simple conceal-ment spell. The shifters smelled Charles' kind abstractly, but not directly. Why? Because they were perched up in the trees. As the spell withered away, I couldn't help but laugh.

A middle-aged man in black spandex clung to the trunk halfway up. He had a surprised expression mingled with an "oh crap" look.

"Gotcha!" I yelled up at him.

He tried to jump away into the trees, but I threw some binding around him and watched as he fell to the ground to a lump. Charles was standing over him with a sword a moment later. "How do ya like me now?"

"Except I was the one that did it, dummy," I said. "C'mon, grab him. We'll take him in and see if Jonas hit the toilet or something."

Now we had two sources of information, and I knew very well that Toa and Dominicous would work them off of each other.

I'd been on the job for all of fifteen minutes and already I'd found one of the bad guys. Was I good, or was I good.

I couldn't help the strut back to the house as Charles carried the guy. If there was trouble coming, a body torn up by having kids wasn't enough to prevent me from meeting the danger. And since my kids were taken care of, even if the worst happened, I could continue to protect them, and our way of life, without reservation.

I smiled in elation as I walked inside and gestured back to Charles. "Got one."

I felt pride well up through my link with Stefan. Yup, I was back.

"What should we do with him—"

Charles was cut off by a harried shifter bursting through the door in sweats. His gaze swept the room until he honed in on Tim. "Jim was taken down at the south end. It smelled like their kind." No one had to question which kind "their kind" was, even though he didn't flick his eyes at Stefan or anyone else.

"Is he dead?" Tim asked, standing up in a rush.

"Yes. And there was blood left behind, along with Jonas' scent."

Tim's expression found Stefan, who was now standing with a blank face. Cold washed through my body. "Did someone go look for him?" I asked with a calm voice. There was no need to freak out yet.

Al, the shifter who had discovered the body, looked at me with a grim face. "The blood dripped along drag marks and went deep into the trees. Then the impression of footfall became heavier and the drag marks vanished. He was carried at the end. I doubt he was conscious."

Now it was time to freak out.

I ran out the door and around the building, Stefan and Charles right behind me, a pack of shifters following them. With Al's lead, we found the spot in question and I let my magic blanket the area, reading the traces of the invisibility spell as well as a binding spell. The magic work wasn't intricate, but it was worked with a practiced hand.

"Why would they take Jonas but leave a shifter?" I asked with a flat voice, pushing through the trees with Stefan beside me.

"Do you feel anything?" Stefan asked.

"Just remnants of magic. It's already vanishing back into nature. No one's around. They took off."

"Jonas?"

I shook my head. If he wasn't working magic, I wouldn't find him.

Stefan stepped in front, eyes to the ground. He kept moving at a quick pace, using his eyes, his magic, and sense of smell to track. In a hundred yards we reached a small dirt road with fresh spots of blood, a large area of flattened grass where a body had probably been thrown on the ground, and tire tracks.

Someone had taken Jonas. We had their shifter, so they took my bodyguard and then left their man behind when they realized we had him, too. "And they are all going to die," I said with clenched teeth, finishing my thought.

Stefan turned toward me with a mask of rage taking over his expression. His eyes burned and his body was flexed, an alpha ready to take on an army. "Yes, they will. C'mon, we have work to do."

Pushing down the well of emotion, and strapping on rage like Stefan, I gave a quick glance at the grim-faced and equally pissed Charles before I followed Stefan back into the trees. They'd declared war by trying to kill me, and just put a time stamp on it by taking Jonas—it was time to respond. And I'd make sure our answer was gruesome. No one messed with my family and walked away. I'd make sure of that.

_*_*_*_*_*_*_*_*_*_*_

Thank you for taking the time to read my ebook.

Check out Jonas (book 7):

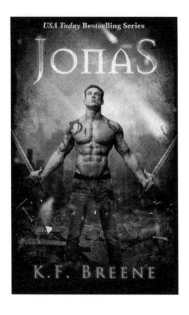

Never   miss   a   new   release   or   sale: http://eepurl.com/F3kmT

WEBSITE: KFBREENE.COM
    Facebook: www.facebook.com/authorKF
    Fan and Social Group: https://goo.gl/KAgoNr
    Twitter: @KFBreene

REVIEW IT. PLEASE SUPPORT THE BOOK AND HELP OTHERS by telling them what you liked by reviewing on Amazon or Goodreads or other stores. If you do write a review, please send me an email to let me know (KFBreene@gmail.com) so I can   thank   you   personally!   Or   visit   me   at http://www.kfbreene.com.

LEND IT! ALL MY BOOKS ARE LENDING-ENABLED. PLEASE share with your friends.

RECOMMEND IT. IF YOU THINK SOMEONE ELSE MIGHT LIKE this book, please help pass the title along to friends, readers' groups, or discussions.

JONAS (BOOK 7)

Sasha's journey continues in:

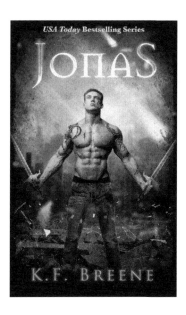

Chapter I

Jonas blinked his eyes open and minutely shook his head. Throbs of pain pulsed behind his forehead. He felt rough stone under his bruised knees. His wrists were secured behind his back with unyielding metal. Pulling his arms apart, then twisting, had the shackles biting into his skin. A trickle of liquid dribbled into his palm. Blood.

He remembered feeling eyes on him at the *Mata* compound. The feeling of being watched had tickled between his shoulder blades. He'd looked around, then behind him, to see if one of the mangy shifters was staring at him. Except for a distant wolf at the far end of the perimeter, though, no one had been around.

He'd recalled the tricks of magic that could make a person invisible two seconds before a rough voice said, "Don't kill him—we can use him." Something dull had crashed down on his head before all went dark. Only someone with advanced use of magic could create and use an invisibility spell. Plus, that accent had been English. Jonas didn't know much about that pansy country, but he knew the irritating speech when he heard it.

It seemed they had out-of-town visitors. Probably here to cash in on all the problems with the Council. He couldn't blame them—he'd heard that Cato had tried a similar take-over method when the English and French were battling each other. He couldn't blame them, but he could sure kill them for thinking his country was defenseless.

As soon as he got free, that was.

Jonas looked around. He knelt in the middle of a square room made of old stone. Mold grew in cracks on the walls and across the floor. A damp, musty smell lingered in the air. There was one window, way up high at the top of the far wall, indicating most of this room was underground. An old basement probably, and not even remotely close to the health code standards.

Jonas heaved a laugh. He wiggled his arms again, hearing the clink of chain. He tried to move his feet, half-numb from being in this position for however long, and heard the same jingle. He was probably secured to the floor. His torso leaned against a thin strip of metal—a bar that made up a side of a rectangle. The two ends were braced into the floor to hold him up. Awfully nice of them, giving him something to lean on. He wondered why he wasn't secured to that, though.

There was a stone seat next to the wall in front of him, and one on the side. The other wall was bare. He glanced behind him. In the back, right corner was a stand gleaming with well-polished tools. Flays, whips, paddles, spikes—this was the makings for a great time. Jonas had a similar array in his quarters at the Mansion.

As a smile graced his lips for the shock the torturer would get when his version of torture wasn't going according to plan, the door behind him opened with a metallic wheeze. Two clicks announced someone in high heels before the door latched, the metallic sound echoing through the chamber. Soft leather slid against wood, which clinked off of metal, in that back corner.

The torturer had arrived. And it was either a cross-dressing male, or a female.

He would have fun with either.

The clicks sounded again, coming around his body and stopping directly in front of him. A female, small for one of their kind, stood in front of him with a blank expression that didn't adequately hide the tightness around her eyes. She wore a red leather corset, black fishnet stockings, and shiny black heels. A pony tail held her glossy brown hair high on her head. Expertly manicured fingernails clutched her weapon of choice, a whip. Her features were straight and dainty, and her lips were a plump, bright red. She would be really hot if she wasn't trying too hard—if the female was any more rigid, she'd have to pull the stick out of her ass to sit down.

She obviously felt inadequate in what she wore, but that hold on the whip gave Jonas shivers. Very pleasant shivers. She balanced it delicately in a sure, comfortable grip. Confidence radiated in the light touch she had with that weapon. The expertly-worked leather was well-maintained—probably oiled and looked after on a regular basis. It would slash and cut in all the right ways.

Jonas let his gaze drift back up to her face. Her eyes were a clear blue and sparkling with intelligence. Currently, she was surveying his body and tracing his scars with her gaze. Trying to find his weaknesses. Trying to figure out how hard he really was—how easily he would break.

He'd been the subject of this type of scrutiny his whole life. Only, usually the one in control wore a sneer. In contrast, the gleam in her eyes bent more toward analysis.

Jonas felt a thrill of anticipation. So few females knew how to properly dominate. So few people in general, actually, females or males. He'd really only found one who could take him away from the encroaching wildness in his emotions and reset him. Make him someone that could exist with others without randomly sticking knives in people or throwing them through walls. But she had to struggle to dominate him on a regular basis. She wasn't as strong as she pretended to be, and she didn't understand the hardware as well as she needed to.

Most people probably didn't look forward to a torture session like he was. But by the look of it, this female could handle that whip. And he wanted to see what she was made of. He had a feeling she was a natural, and his experienced eye told him she'd had a lot of practice. Two good things.

As the heat started to burn in him, he recognized a

shadow slowly creep into her gaze. The sparkle in her eyes started to ebb. Her body stiffened even more.

His arousal made her uncomfortable. Yet... she was wearing a corset. And liked to play with whips. What was this female playing at?

Jonas filed that information away as she started to speak in a low, sensual voice. "By now I imagine you know you've been taken. All we require out of you is information. Just a few easy answers and everyone is happy. You don't need to see me any more than is absolutely necessary."

She paused expectantly. Jonas simply stared. He was getting bored.

"So let's start with the easy ones, shall we?" She sauntered closer. As her shoes clicked on the stone she snaked the whip over her shoulder and then down across her body, eyeing the places on his torso her first strikes would land. That leather traveled over well-rounded breasts and delicious cleavage before sliding down her flat stomach and over shapely thighs. She was getting ready, not trying to entice him sexually. Her brutality was coming to the surface.

Jonas' heart started to hammer. That light of confident ruthlessness sparkled in her eyes as she ran her finger lightly over the handle of her whip. Her pink tongue ran over that sensuous bottom lip before she smiled a little to herself. She was probably planning to punish him for his earlier arousal— probably going to teach him a lesson.

Oh gods, he really hoped she was planning to punish him. For a long time. Really hard.

He opened and closed his fists in anticipation.

"What's your name?" she asked in a sultry voice.

Jonas let his gaze burn into hers. Without flinching, tightness around her eyes completely gone, rigidity having melted in a graceful sensuousness that could not be taught, she met his gaze with a wild streak of raw violence. This female was stepping onto the battle field and her energy soaked into him like a power line. Jonas' dick was so hard he was having trouble thinking.

"I usually will not ask a question twice without something to fill the pauses. However, since this is your first time, I'll be lenient. Just this once." She stopped right in front of him. Her whip dangled down her thigh. "What is your name?"

Jonas watched her blue eyes flash. *Here it comes.*

She moved with the grace of a predator. Her hand came up quickly and *flicked.* The whip splashed out in a string of leather and licked his torso. A stinging pain he barely registered lanced his pec. She was taking it easy on him.

Damn.

"What is your name?" she asked again. He could hear the passion in her voice. The desire to inflict pain humming deeply in her words. But when the next lash fell, it was barely harder than the last.

His ardor started to drain away in his disappointment. She should've been able to tell what he could take by sizing him up—any torturer worthy of the title had that trait. And she probably did notice it—it seemed like she had by that analytical gaze—but she didn't act on it. She had the ability, but not the gumption.

What damned, depressing news.

Jonas let his gaze drift straight-ahead toward the wall. Her sensual voice droned on as Jonas let his mind drift to Sasha and the Boss. He wondered how the little babies were. He wasn't a people person, but he'd always loved kids. They were so sweet and innocent when they were young. They looked at the world with big, bright eyes. Anything was possible. Jonas really wanted his own someday. He wanted a mate he could protect and support. A family to raise and a home away from the Mansion where he could spend his dawnings. He wanted peace, both of mind and body. Tranquility.

A whip stroke fell, the slice across his chest barely registering. He completely ignored any that came after—it wasn't hard to do.

He thought back to holding Sabrina when she was just a few hours old. He'd almost felt that tranquility he craved. That deeper purpose. Looking on her tiny, angelic face, he'd let go of his own demons. All he could think about was wanting to give everything he had to make sure Sasha's two infants went through life with the best it had to offer. They wouldn't be picked on and torn apart like he was. They'd have someone to stand up for them—to protect them, even if their parents took off. Jonas would make sure they were nothing but loved and supported, no matter what came.

The bite of the leather sank in a little deeper. Not just a housefly, now. A horse fly. Still irritating. He almost wanted to tell her to just move on to a knife—she wasn't fulfilling his expectations with the whip.

"Just your name. That's all I want."

He barely stopped himself from rolling his eyes as he let the caress of the leather lull his mind. Every torturer wanted to break their subject. That was the point. The beginning was an answer to a simple question. Just one answer. That wasn't so bad, the subject would think. The reprieve of pain would be a nice change. Then the next answer. And the next. When the pain got really bad, those answers were a lifeline until suddenly, the tortured was nothing more than a broken snitch. He was a dog, trained to obey.

That just didn't fly with Jonas. Plus, he'd been through all this before. It hadn't mattered that the boys who caught him were just pretending—their knives were real. The blood and pain was real. And he'd squealed. He'd squealed like a little pig. He'd told on his good friend for taking Julia's sword. He'd told on himself for a million things he shouldn't have done. He'd made stuff up. He'd pissed himself. He'd cried and begged. He'd promised them he'd do anything, *anything* if they'd let him go.

He'd been twelve. A child. The boys had been graduating school—much older than him. He'd been their first victim and he'd had to endure five different sessions before they'd gotten bored with him. They'd gotten caught when the next boy told on them. The other boy hadn't been afraid to speak up and became an instant martyr. Instead of shunning him, the adults all thought he was brave for enduring the torture.

No one ever knew Jonas had endured worse. He'd been too embarrassed to say anything.

"That's all for today. Tomorrow maybe you'll come to your senses."

It took Jonas a moment to realize the light pain had stopped. He looked around in confusion, only catching the female wiping off her whip at the far wall and hanging it up carefully. He glanced down at his chest. He had two gashes, and a great many welts.

The pain of his memories was what lingered, however. Physical pain would diminish in time. His past wouldn't. And hadn't.

Buy it now: Jonas

ABOUT THE AUTHOR

K.F. Breene is a USA TODAY BESTSELLING author of the Darkness Series and Warrior Chronicles. She lives in wine country where over every rolling hill, or behind every cow, an evil sorcerer might be plotting his next villainous deed while holding a bottle of wine and brick of cheese. Her husband thinks she's cracked for wandering around, muttering about magic and swords. Her kids are on board with her fantastical imagination, except when the description of the monsters becomes too real.

She'll wait until they're older to tell them that monsters are real, and so is the magic to fight them. She wants them to sleep through the night, after all...

Never miss the next monster! Sign up here!

Join the reader group to chat with her personally: https://goo.gl/KAgoNr

Contact info:
kfbreene.com/
kfbreene@gmail.com

OTHER TITLES BY K.F. BREENE

Never want to miss the latest? Sign up here!

Check out her website: kfbreene.com

Made in the USA
Middletown, DE
14 September 2020

19590030R00094